ATTACK on TITAN

BEFORE THE FALL

CREATED BY HAJIME ISAYAMA
A NOVEL BY RYO SUZUKAZE
ART BY THORES SHIBAMOTO

Can mankind's ingenuity stand up against the Titans?

Attack on Titan
Before the Fall

Created by Hajime Isayama
A Novel by Ryo Suzukaze
Art by THORES Shibamoto

Translated by Ko Ransom

VERTICAL.

Art by Thores Shibamoto.

Originally published in Japanese as *Shingeki no Kyojin: Before the Fall.*

This is a work of fiction.

ISBN: 978-1-939130-86-0

Manufactured in the United States of America

First Edition

Vertical, Inc.
451 Park Avenue South
7th Floor
New York, NY 10016
www.vertical-inc.com

CONTENTS

PROLOGUE

The high-pitched bell rang out against a dark gray sky. Liberty Bell—a name familiar to every resident of Shiganshina District. The bronze bell that hung over the impressively solid, fifty-meter-tall Wall Maria was a town symbol. While it was originally made for use in emergencies and disasters, it had, fortunately, never been used a single time for that purpose.

Though it was not particularly bright out, Angel Aaltonen shaded his eyes with his hand as he looked up to the towering, cliff-like Wall Maria. While you could never forget about its incredible size, being close to it only made its enormity more prominent. The Wall had such an overwhelming presence that it could even inspire awe to the point where it was deified by some. In a world devoid of a god to pray to, the Wall was the only existence that one could take solace in.

Of course, when Wall Maria was first built, it was not in order to be a religious object. Its reason for existing was clear: to protect against outside enemies. In other words, a menace that threatened mankind existed outside the Wall. Terrifying monsters that necessitated a gigantic wall.

"Eh. Who knows if they really even exist or not."

Angel scowled, slightly distorting his slender face as he violently scratched his head, disheveled hair and all. While his hair would shine gold if he were to take care of it, its color was hopelessly dull, perhaps because of his thoroughly hands-off approach. It was not just his hair, either—his life of shutting himself inside his workshop and spending all day creating military equipment seemed to have made his face pale to the point where his colleagues openly called him "pasty."

Though he looked unhealthy, and while it was true that he lived an unhealthy life, Angel's body was surprisingly robust. That much was clear even when he had his work clothes on. His body had been forged

9

through the natural course of his work. The vitality that pervaded his body was befitting of an eighteen-year-old male such as himself.

"If only that wall were a little lower…"

"You'd be able to peek over it?"

Angel didn't even turn as he smirked at the quiet voice behind him.

"If something's hidden from you, it makes you want to peek."

"Is that how men are?"

"That's just curiosity."

As he mumbled, Angel glanced at the profile of the woman who now stood beside him.

The woman coolly gazing at Wall Maria was known as Maria Carlstedt. Her dignified, elegant figure seemed impeccable, an impression only reinforced by the soldier's uniform she managed to wear with style. An emblem of a rose, the sign of the Garrison, was drawn on her khaki jacket, and one could see in her a pride and confidence she held for her job. Her shining, tied black hair served as a sign of her resolve.

"Don't do anything that'll make you stand out. It'll be a pain if the Military Police Brigade sets their eyes on you."

"Are you warning me as a soldier?"

"I'm advising you as your childhood friend."

It had started to become a taboo to have an interest in the outside world. Any conspicuous actions could mark you as a suspicious individual in the eyes of the Military Police Brigade.

They ought to just release the information.

While interest would surely fade if the royal government made public the information they held about what was outside the Wall, there must have been some group out there who profited from this ignorance and thus kept the truth a secret.

"You know, I'm running into trouble at work because of that thing."

"We wouldn't even be able to live our lives without the Walls, though," reminded Maria.

Her face was full of pride as she looked up at the wall. For her, a member of the Garrison, Wall Maria was, without question, a special structure. The Garrison's primary duties involved addressing the needs of the walled cities, as well as reinforcing and repairing the Walls, mankind's most vital military installation.

But unlike Maria, Angel did not hold any special attachment for the Walls.

A wall is a wall.

Angel's conclusion came from the fact that his livelihood involved developing and manufacturing arms to be sold to the military corps.

The best defense is a good offense.

He did not voice his thoughts, though. He doubted that Maria would agree with him if he were to, and he could see that any argument with her would never reach a conclusion. In fact, they had talked about the subject more than once in the past, and Angel had been left with the bitter experience of being harshly argued into a corner every time.

"And by the way, what's with your hair?" Maria sighed as she used her hands to comb through Angel's unkempt head.

"H-Hey! I'm not a kid, cut it out."

Angel became flustered, concerned about what those around him would think, but Maria utterly ignored him.

"If you're not a kid, then don't give me so much trouble."

"Okay, okay."

"And don't forget to shave."

Having fixed his hair to her liking, Maria began to circle around Angel, checking his appearance, then gave a single, satisfied nod.

"Shouldn't you be working, by the way?"

"I'm just off the night shift. Listen, I'm not skipping work." Maria scowled at Angel, almost as if to add an *unlike you*.

"Oh, so you're here to see Solm back. Looks like you two are getting along."

"Same with you, right?"

"I don't remember ever getting engaged to Solm," Angel mumbled.

Maria wordlessly scowled, then said, "Allow me to rephrase. I guess you two are best friends of sorts."

As Angel and Maria were busy chatting, the area around Wall Maria's main gate began to bustle with activity. Soon, the space was jammed full of people. Perhaps they had assembled because they heard the sound of the bell. A quick glance showed there to be around three hundred people. Young and old, male and female, they were all gathered there for the same reason as Angel. Soon, the Survey Corps would return from an expedition outside the Wall. They would be passing through the main gate and returning to their barracks riding northward on one of the avenues, but the scene, thanks to the soldiers' brave figures, made their return seem almost like a celebratory parade. As the residents of Shiganshina District had little to amuse themselves with, the return had become somewhat of a special event.

Or I guess that's how it was in the past...

While it looked as though many people were present on first glance, it was actually little more than a local gathering. Considering that Shiganshina District's population was a little over thirty thousand, one might conclude that the Survey Corps' return was not a matter of interest to the district's residents. What's more, over half of the crowd consisted of hecklers. Other than the soldiers' relatives, few had any emotional attachment to their return.

Then again, the residents' cold response was only natural.

They don't release their information. They can't show their results. And despite that, their expeditions are funded by tax money...

It seemed as though some sort of political decision was the only thing keeping the Survey Corps alive in spite of the people's dissatisfaction. Many parts of the Survey Corps' expeditions were opaque, and the residents had absolutely no way of knowing anything about the backroom politics that went on.

"It's about time for our heroes to make their grand return."

While the Wall kept them from being able to see the heroic figure cut by the Survey Corps, they could hear a rhythmical sound coming from the other side. It was the beat made by dozens of galloping warhorses. The soldiers' movements seemed to grow more hurried as they heard the noise. Perhaps it was their regular training, but they made no wasted movements, working in a systematic, almost mechanical way. This systematic approach was exactly what was needed, as the gate had to be opened and closed quickly.

"I just hope it went well," Maria said nervously.

"Are you talking about their mission?"

"What else is there?"

"It's not like their results are what really matters to you."

"That's not true," Maria said nonchalantly, though there was no way she was being honest. She had to have been worried about the safety of Solm, her fiancée. The Survey Corps' mission could mean little to her.

Of course, I guess I'm the same way.

The life of his best friend was a far larger concern to Angel than the results of a mission clouded in mystery.

"Aren't you straight-laced."

"Yeah, when I have this uniform on."

As Angel and Maria traded barbs, the Survey Corps closed in on their destination. With numerous horses kicking at the ground, the earth faintly shook.

The soldier standing atop the lookout post gave the command. "Open the gate! Open the gate!" Moments later, the giant gate, nearly ten meters in height, began to open with a deafening roar. Angel squinted and bent forward, focusing his vision on the world he could see beyond the gate.

All I can make out is barren earth.

Though he searched, Angel could find nothing worth special mention. Then, before he had a chance for any further observation, the outside world was covered in dirt kicked up by the horses.

Too bad there aren't any of those monsters that you hear about.

Rather than monsters, all Angel could see was a pack of horses. Riding them were hooded cavalry who wore cloaks emblazoned with wings—Survey Corps soldiers.

Putting aside their reputation, they do look the part.

The cavalry passing through the gate one after another made a stunning impression.

"Close the gate! Close the gate!"

As soon as the Survey Corps had passed through, the gate was briskly shut. It was an admirably quick job. The gate had been open for a minute at most, showing the Garrison's firm resolve to keep any outside enemies from invading. Maria looked faintly proud.

But while the Garrison had carried out its duties perfectly, the Survey Corps seemed sullen.

"They lost a lot of men…"

About fifty soldiers had returned. A force of almost eighty had left for the half-day expedition, but despite the mission's short length, they had suffered major losses. Nor did the surviving soldiers return unharmed. Most of them only had minor wounds, but some had lost limbs. Others returned as corpses.

I don't know what their goal was, but it looks like another failed expedition.

He could tell by the extent of the losses, as well as the soldiers' dour looks. It seemed as though the residents may have thought the same, as there were few cheers. The mood of the scene was hardly celebratory, but at the same time, there was no sense of disappointment. The people must not have expected anything from the Survey Corps to begin with.

I guess the best way to not be let down is to have low expectations from the outset.

Sighing, Angel checked the faces of each of the returning soldiers. Every one of the valiant Survey Corps soldiers wore a fearless expression. Among them was a handsome man whom he recognized.

Solm Hume. He was a young, rising star in the Survey Corps as well as Angel's childhood friend.

He's really turned into a lady-killer, huh.

Solm's face was dirty with soot and dust, but he didn't seem to be injured. His sharp gaze was focused straight ahead as he walked his horse, skillfully controlling its reins in his hands.

"I guess he wouldn't die off *that* easily."

"Of course not. He can't leave me as a widow before we're even married."

"You should really get him to request a change of assignment soon. We might not be laughing about this for long."

"Maybe if he was the kind of person who listened to others…"

"True," Angel laughed bitterly. "For now, then, let's just be happy that he made a safe return."

Though Angel and Maria were celebrating Solm's return, the families of the soldiers who didn't make it back were overwhelmed with grief. There was always the possibility that a soldier would never return from an expedition. Soldiers knew this when they chose to go on one, as well as their families.

Still, they must not have thought that they would really die.

That much was clear from their confusion and panic. In particular, a woman wearing maternity clothes drew Angel's attention. She looked to be around twenty years old. She was fair-skinned and delicate, and seemed so wan that she might fall over without any support.

Maria looked on with concern at the woman who wandered from place to place like a ghost.

"Someone you know?"

"Yes. That's Elena Mansell. Her husband is Team Leader Heath."

"Solm's superior, then."

Angel had never met the man before, so the name brought no face to mind. Nevertheless, if he was a team leader, he had to have been a talented soldier even among the Survey Corps.

"So Team Leader Heath didn't make it back. Poor thing, they just got married…" Maria said with a pained look.

I see, could be you tomorrow…

Elena was approaching soldiers with her faltering steps to ask each of them if her now-departed husband was "safe." Her eyes were blank and unfocused.

"The royal government's going to take care of her, right?"

"She shouldn't have any trouble making ends meet."

"You can't replace a husband with money alone, though."

"I just wish there was something I could do."

"Yeah…"

Anything they could do, though, would be of little importance.

Never mind the money, all she'd want is her husband back.

15

No matter what they did, they wouldn't be able to help Elena.

I guess time is the only cure…

As Angel was thinking, an explosion roared out above his head like a clap of thunder. The air shook slightly from the impact. Instinctively, Angel flinched, but he saw no signs of lightning around him.

"What just happened?!"

As if to answer, the faint smell of chemicals wafted in the air, carried by the south wind.

"That's…"

As Angel's nose twitched, it picked up the traces of the chemical ingredients that tinged the air around him.

Saltpeter, charcoal, sulfur, aluminum…

In other words, gunpowder.

"Did they fire off a cannon?"

He couldn't see from his position on the street, but he was certain, and for a simple reason.

So that's where they put the cannons I made, up there on the wall.

Angel had created ten cannons after receiving an order from the military corps, but he was never told how they would be used. After hearing the explosion overhead, though, he knew that they had been put atop Wall Maria.

"What was that bombardment?"

"Probably a warning shot."

"So those Titans we've heard so much about have decided to pay us a visit."

"Titan" was the generic name given to the monsters that preyed upon humans. Mankind had been forced to construct giant walls and to live inside of them in order to escape the threat posed by the Titans. It must have been the Titans that inflicted the massive losses on the Survey Corps during its expedition.

I wish I could see them once, though. Just for future reference.

While it was easy to imagine the Titans as terrible monstrosities, Angel was not particularly scared of them. He couldn't be frightened by something that he only knew of conceptually. To Angel, Titans were like formless ghosts.

"But what an awful sound…"

Angel scowled at the echoes of the cannons firing in succession as he covered both ears with his hands.

I wouldn't be surprised if they ordered suppressors next.

The sound of a tenth cannon shot ripped through the air right as Angel smiled wryly, but that was the end of the bombardment.

"Did they kill them?"

Angel timidly took his hands off his ears as he looked at Maria.

"It'd be nice if they did, but I doubt it."

"You do, huh…" Angel mumbled as he focused his sight on Wall Maria. If they had fired ten whole shots, it wouldn't matter if they had landed a direct hit on any of the Titans. There would be a sea of fire around them. No living creature could survive in it.

Anything that was alive down there is sure to have died instantly.

No matter how unexpectedly monstrous the Titans were, the cannons still had enough firepower to take them out.

One roasted Titan, hot and ready.

But then, as if to crush Angel's pride, footfalls began to close in from the other side of the Wall.

"You can't be serious…"

"The Titans probably got too close to the Wall," Maria coolly explained to Angel while his mouth hung agape.

"So that's why they stopped firing."

Wall Maria, sometimes called indestructible, had yet to allow the Titans in. It was thick enough to deflect any of the Titans' strikes, and tall enough to be too high to scale.

"The way you're talking, it sounds like you knew that this would happen."

"Better that than to mess up and accidentally damage the Wall."

"As the person who made those cannons, though, I'm a little conflicted…"

Angel clenched his fist.

Still, if that's what their footsteps sound like…

Angel doubted his own ears. The roaring sound of the steadily approaching footfalls in no way resembled human steps. It was like the sound of an earthquake, and in truth, the ground faintly rumbled. It was proof of the Titans' unbelievably large size.

They're like walking disasters.

As soon as he compared them to natural threats, the once vague, ghost-like Titans suddenly seemed more real. Titans weren't imaginary monsters. They were real dangers to mankind. Angel's personal definition of the Titans was quickly rewritten, but as soon as it was, a shiver ran through his body. A cold sweat ran down his back, he broke out in goose bumps, and deep inside his chest, he felt his heart begin to pound. His instincts were sounding a warning.

Step by step, the Titan continued to approach, accompanied by a quaking sound. Despite the sluggish cow-like pace, the distance between Angel and the Titan shrank slowly but surely.

The Titan's footsteps suddenly stopped. Perhaps the Wall had gotten in its path.

It's about to attack.

Angel steeled himself and focused his senses on the Titan's movements but picked up close to nothing.

"It's not doing anything?" Angel furrowed his brow. "I was sure it was going to try to break down the Wall."

This belief, however, was probably nothing more than the result of an ignorant bias, and Angel must have projected his own images of how a Titan would act onto the one on the other side of the Wall.

I suppose if they really were smart enough to be able to do something to the Wall, mankind would already be extinct.

Angel looked up at the towering Wall Maria.

"Thanks be to Wall Maria, I see."

"Have you started to get a better idea of why this is here?"

"A better idea than I had wanted."

"Do you still think that the best defense is a good offense?"

"Aren't you a mean one."

"Yeah, sometimes."

Angel shrugged his shoulders at Maria as she grinned. His nerves had calmed a bit, perhaps due to their exchange. The people of the town, too, had started to recover from the shock of the sudden bombardment. Some may have even mistook it as celebrating the Survey Corps' return.

"Why don't we go see Solm."

Right as Maria spoke, a single drop of rain hit Angel's cheek. He wiped his face with the back of his hand and looked up at the sky. It was covered in thick clouds that seemed ready to burst.

"So it really does rain when people are grieving."

"Looks like we might get some showers…"

Blocking out the sun's rays with her hand, Maria looked at the gray sky. It had started to sprinkle. At this rate, there would be a downpour soon.

We should probably get moving.

Right as Angel thought this, a black, round object entered his field of vision.

"A bird?" Angel thought for a moment, but he immediately changed his mind. No bird was that round.

"Dodge!!"

The sudden voice that shouted down from above froze Angel's body. The shout had come from a Garrison soldier on top of the wall.

Dodge?!

He must have been referring to the black, spherical mass, but Angel couldn't tell what kind of dangerous object it could have been. Even if he could, he didn't have enough time to react. The mass fell toward, then crashed into the stone pavement a few meters in front of him.

"Take cover!!"

Angel and Maria both flattened themselves on the ground. While it still could have been some sort of bomb, the mass splattered like a ripened fruit, spraying the area with whatever unknown substance was inside.

"That's…"

It had been flattened by the impact, but they could tell what the fallen object was.

"It's…a head…"

While it barely resembled its original shape, it was still clear. Its eye sockets were sunken in, its nose had been sliced off, and its mouth was still visible despite having no lower jaw. Its hair must have made it look black as it flew through the air, and the substance that had come from it was some sort of mixture of brains, bone fragments, and bodily fluids. The unbearably gruesome sight caused the contents of Angel's stomach to climb back into his throat. The moment his stomach juices spread across his mouth, Angel covered it with his hand and retched, though he somehow managed to keep from vomiting.

"What… What's going on?"

As he stood confused, a woman approached him with an unsteady gait. It was Elena.

"Oh, so this is where you were dawdling?"

Elena walked up to the severed head and crouched down with no regard for the filth that would get on her dress. She peeled the head off of the ground it clung to, then held it to her bosom.

"No wonder you were late."

Elena let out a grotesque cackle.

"Is that…her husband's?"

"I'd have to check to make sure, but I'm pretty sure it is…"

Elena continued to mumble toward the hunk of flesh, apparently unable to register his death.

But why would a head come from the sky?

When Angel looked up, searching for an answer, he saw something that made his eyes grow wide. Countless severed heads were flying through the sky like shooting stars. One distorted flower after another bloomed on the ground as the heads flew in from outside the Wall. As this happened, screams started to come from all around.

"Are Titans throwing the heads over?"

It was strange, but the bizarre situation would then make sense.

"But why heads…"

"There's no reason."

"What do you mean?"

"They eat because they want to. They throw away what they don't like. That's it."

"But then—"

Angel was about to continue, "They're no different from humans," but he swallowed his words. He couldn't allow himself to admit something like that. As he struggled to deepen his understanding of the Titans' actions, more heads continued to rain down.

"Damn it! Do they think they're playing horseshoes or something?!" Angel cursed as he spit each word out.

Fortunately, no one was hurt by the heads, but the ground and nearby structures were now filthy, stained with splattered brains, bodily fluids, and chunks of meat. The scene was so repulsive that it felt otherworldly.

The hellish image must have struck fear in the people. The crowd that had assembled to celebrate the Survey Corps' return was now scattering in confusion, screaming. It was a natural reaction to an event as unimaginable as human heads raining from the sky.

The heads eventually stopped, either out of choice or because there were none left to throw. Still, the people had been gripped by fear, and it was only a matter of time before they would be in a state of panic.

You think you can just do whatever you want?

Even Angel wasn't able to keep calm, but there was one group that could and did. The Survey Corps. They stood firm and unflinching despite the horrifying spectacle that was taking place before them. It was proof of their intense training, as well as of the many other difficulties even crueler than this that they had overcome.

But even among these courageous soldiers, one man stood especially tall.

Jorge Piquer.

The statuesque, majestic man was a squad leader in the Survey Corps. Jorge grabbed a flare gun from his waist, pointed it to the sky, then pulled the trigger without hesitation. A flash of light shot out from the muzzle, accompanied by a report. A bright light like the sun itself came from the shot as it exploded in mid-air.

"A White Star…"

The charge that had been loaded into the flare gun was known as a White Star. While it was normally used for illumination at night and as a signal to other soldiers, it was now being used to draw the attention of the panicking city residents. They stopped in place, all looking up to the light in the sky.

For a moment, everything around was quiet. Jorge jumped on this opportunity and went into action.

"Calm down! Calm down!!"

His voice, even louder than the flare gun's report, spread through the people to incredible effect. One after another, they began to come back to their senses, as if he had exorcised them of a demon. For a man used to commanding groups of brave soldiers, striking sense into regular citizens must have been a simple feat. While the scene had turned into an unexpected display of the Survey Corps' prowess, now was hardly the time or place for a celebration of their return.

The dripping rain gradually began coming down harder, surely to help wash away the scattered brains.

CHAPTER ONE

The year 743.

Mankind was facing the danger of extinction at the hands of the Titans that had suddenly appeared at the center stage of history. Where had they come from, and what was their purpose? Some said that they were natural disasters, while others insisted that they were divine retribution. Either way, mankind had been reduced to simple, clueless prey whose total population had plummeted to 500,000.

Humanity had moved to living inside the walled cities because there was no other way to resist the Titans. In other words, humanity avoided the worst of all outcomes, extinction, by deciding to become a species of caged birds. Mankind had been given 720,000 square kilometers to live in. While the soil was hardly fertile, there was at least enough space to live a modest existence. Encircling the area was the key wall of the walled cities—Wall Maria. The firm wall stood fifty meters tall and stretched for a total of 3,200 kilometers, perfectly isolating the interior from invading Titans.

Wall Maria was not the only wall. Waiting a hundred kilometers farther in was a second wall, Wall Rose, and past that was Wall Sheena, the last line of defense. These three protective walls allowed humanity to regain peace, though it was a temporary one.

Even now, a little over thirty years after the Titans appeared, Titans and humans still stood as predators and prey. The Titans' behavior remained full of mysteries. Little was known about them other than the fact that they preyed on humans. The worst part of it all was that they did not know the Titans' weakness. Humanity had yet to win a battle against the Titans, and it was now common knowledge that the Titans were immortal. Only having gleaned that much in more than a quarter-century was quite shabby, but it was no surprise as people had not been aggressive in surveying or investigating the Titans.

No need to take back the outside world.

Live happily while you can.

An unwritten code, that mankind was fated to live as caged birds, had spread among the people.

***

Shiganshina District was located at the southernmost edge of Wall Maria. It was a strangely built town, jutting out from the wall like a growth. Its structure seemed unthinkable if one took into consideration the fact that Titans roamed around the area outside of the wall, but in fact, it was built this way out of logical defensive reasons. While the Garrison was skilled at its job, patrolling all of Wall Maria with about ten thousand troops was not a realistic option. From this reality came the idea of drawing the Titans in. Having a town protrude from the wall and settling people there would naturally cause the Titans to gather toward their human prey. Attracting the Titans to a limited area made patrolling Wall Maria easier and allowed the Garrison to focus its strength. In other words, the residents of Shiganshina District were bait, and the Titans were like fish that swarmed to them.

This groundbreaking idea, however, wouldn't work unless people actually lived in the town. Shiganshina District's residents lived there knowing the risks because the royal government offered them tax benefits. This was enough to cause a stream of people to fill the town regardless of the risks.

The workshop Angel belonged to stood on the outskirts of Shiganshina District. It had been contracted to develop and manufacture the arms provided to soldiers, and a hundred craftsmen spent their days and nights sweating there.

Three years had already passed since Angel first asked to join the workshop's ranks. He had stood out from the beginning, and he was now both its face and heart. He was nicknamed the master inventor. This, among other things, led to Angel receiving extraordinary treatment despite his young age. Not only did he have a private development lab inside the workshop, he was even allowed to have an assistant.

Still, Angel was not able to fully exercise his talents. The workshop's products were order-made, so there was no way for him to develop equipment according to his own inspiration.

"They should just leave it up to me," Angel sighed, idly scratching his head. "Can't I be allowed to be a little more, uh, flexible?"

While Angel valiantly struggled to express his originality through small twists he'd add to his highly restricted orders, his inability to venture out on his own was a constant source of stress. Delivering a product that deviated just slightly from the order, even if it improved on performance, resulted in him being told to make it over again. His customers looked for arms that fit their initial description, nothing more.

"Ah, welcome back!"

The moment Angel opened the door to his lab, he found himself facing a girl in work clothes.

Corina Ilmari, a craftswoman at the workshop and Angel's assistant. She was eccentric, having come to the workshop simply because she thought herself good with her hands, but she was also a realist who knew that she'd never go hungry doing corps-related work. As an apprentice, she mostly assisted Angel, but she had also made a special place for herself as the male-dominated workshop's mascot. Even craftsmen, who were notoriously unforgiving when dealing with other men, broke into smiles when talking to a fifteen-year-old girl.

I understand how they feel, though.

Angel glanced at Corina. Instead of tools, she held a broom as she bustled about and diligently cleaned the lab. She must have been trying to do something about the cluttered lab while its master was out.

In addition to furniture, such as bookshelves, tables, and a bed, the thirty-square-meter lab also contained equipment needed for development, but the place looked as if a storm had passed through it. Junk that Angel called "inventions" was scattered across the floor, and any furniture functioned as little more than trashcans. While it was known as a development lab, it was also Angel's private room, resulting in a truly chaotic space.

"You look gloomy. Did something happen?" Corina turned her curious, black eyes toward Angel, then suddenly looked startled. "Don't tell me that Solm…"

Angel shook his head before Corina could express her condolences over the loss of a dear friend.

"He wouldn't get himself killed that easily."

"Well, I guess that's true."

"Right?"

"He doesn't seem like the kind of person who'd die. Like you, Angel."

"That's a hell of a way to agree."

Angel put his hand on his forehead and groaned.

"Those Survey Corps guys are definitely no joke. Even so, they were in terrible shape…"

"They were?"

"It started raining soldier heads."

"Excuse me?" Corina yelped as she blinked.

"The Titans threw their leftovers to us from outside the Wall."

Angel sighed then explained what he had just seen, sprinkling in gestures.

"So thanks to them, there's brains all over. All the corps are out right now on cleaning duty."

The rain would help somewhat, but cleaning bits of one's fallen comrades would cause mental anguish to even the most hardened of soldiers. Just thinking about it was enough to turn one's stomach.

"I was right not to go."

"Yup. Still, I think it was good that I was there."

"Why?"

"I was able to really feel how terrifying the Titans are. More motivation to develop arms, right?"

"Maybe, but I still don't want to have to see that…"

"You don't deserve to be called a craftswoman, then."

Corina let out a frustrated groan.

"Speaking of which, I heard the cannons firing. Were they aimed at Titans?"

"Maria said they were warning shots."

"How did it go?"

"Dunno." Angel shrugged. "And that's why we've never been able to make a proper weapon."

"Oh. So is that why you look so gloomy?" Corina clapped her hands together with a satisfied expression.

"I've never seen a Titan before in my life. I don't know how the weapons are being used, and they won't even give me reports, either."

"You aren't getting any feedback."

"Right? If they want to defeat the Titans, they ought to be sharing more information with me."

"Maybe they're not interested in defeating them?"

"It's possible."

It was common knowledge that Titans did not die. Even children knew. It was possible that someone had determined that there was no point in spending resources on trying to kill these immortal Titans. That would explain why they didn't aggressively pursue the development of weapons that could do so.

"If we really investigated their behavior, we should be able to find a weakness or two."

"The whole premise seems to be that they can't be defeated. Overturning it might be hard."

"That's why we should've studied them earlier."

If they could at least understand the nature of their enemies, they would no longer have to be irrationally afraid. But Angel was just a craftsman. Any suggestions he made would be quickly shot down.

That, or they'd call me a political criminal and throw me in prison.

He wasn't even in the position to make a suggestion to the authorities.

As Angel wearily looked overhead, his eyes rested on a plant decorating the room. While he noticed in part because he did not normally have any, it was also just too imposing to ignore. It looked as if it had burst right up through the floor.

"Is that...bamboo?"

The erect rod marked with regular nodes was reminiscent of one, but it was not green like normal bamboo. Its silvery-white color gave it a decidedly metallic appearance. Its leaves were the same color and resembled thin knives.

"What's this?" Angel asked, pointing to the bamboo.

"It's Iron Bamboo," Corina casually replied. "Someone from the Corps brought it here earlier. They want you to see if you can use it as raw material."

"See if I can use it? Isn't it bamboo?"

Angel approached the Iron Bamboo and flicked its stem lightly. It returned a surprisingly metallic sound. It seemed close to the sound given off by bamboo charcoal.

"Has this been processed?" As he touched the Iron Bamboo once again, he felt the trademark coolness of metal.

"It grows naturally in the mountains, apparently."

"I thought ore had to be mined. Since when does it grow out of the ground?"

"I don't know what you're asking me for," Corina mumbled.

No metal would ever grow. Still...

Some species of plants absorbed and stored metals found in the soil. It was possible that Iron Bamboo did so as it grew, accumulating them over many months and years.

I need to do some research at least.

It was true that large amounts of ore slept underground in the mountainous region. Investigating the soil where the Iron Bamboo grew would yield some sort of clue.

"All right, why don't we test it out."

Angel grabbed a dust-covered short sword resting on a shelf. It was one of the standard weapons issued to soldiers.

"Okay, let's see what makes you special."

Angel pulled the blade from its sheath and slashed at the Iron Bamboo with enough force to halve a piece of firewood. A shrill, metallic noise reverberated throughout the room, and a numbing shock ran through the blade.

"That's amazing! You didn't even scratch it!!"

Corina's eyes shone with fascination as she looked closely at the Iron Bamboo. There was a faint streak on its stem, but it was otherwise unchanged. Angel had swung with the intention of slicing it cleanly in two, but the Iron Bamboo was far harder than he'd imagined.

"I see. This does seem like an interesting material to work with."

Angel tossed the chipped blade to the ground.

***

Angel was in the middle of searching for ways to process Iron Bamboo when he was summoned by the workshop chief.

"What a pain…"

Angel let out a deep sigh as he stood in front of the door to the chief's office. Being called by the chief meant one of two things: he was either about to scold you, or force an annoying, difficult job on you. No matter what, it wasn't good.

Angel mumbled hopelessly, scratched his head, and prepared himself for the worst as he opened the door. Unlike Angel's development lab, the chief's room was tidy and neat from corner to corner. Not a single speck of dust was visible on the floor, let alone pieces of junk. Weapons and equipment developed at the workshop neatly lined the room's walls, displaying just how well-organized the workshop chief was.

A table and sofa for visitors dominated the center of the room, and there sat a portly man in work clothes. Caspar Christian, the workshop chief, the only man Angel feared in the workshop, was in his mid-forties and had an intimidating face, a stout body, and healthy, tanned skin. He'd earned fame as a swordsmith, but he would not seem out of place in the Survey Corps. As it was most days, his head was unnecessarily shiny.

"Seems like those cannons you made turned out real good."

Caspar rubbed his shaved head as he began to speak in his dreadful, intimidating voice.

I wonder why it doesn't feel like praise.

Angel couldn't decide if it was because he wasn't used to being lauded or if Caspar's appearance was the problem.

"What was good about them? They couldn't drive the Titans back."

"You were there?"

"My best friend Solm was on the expedition. It's natural that I'd be there for his return, no?"

"I see." Caspar crossed his log-like arms across his chest and nodded, perhaps in assent. "To cut to the chase, looks like the cannons didn't hit the Titans directly."

"What?"

"Seems they weren't quite accurate enough, but the higher-ups are still happy. They want ya to keep up the good work."

"They're happy with defective products? Are you sure this isn't some kind of incredibly backhanded insult?"

"'Course it isn't."

Though Caspar denied it, Angel still found himself unconvinced.

Settling for good enough won't help lead us to the next stage.

Taking verbal abuse would have been easier than this.

"Even if the shells don't hit the Titans spot on, they still do indirect damage, right?"

While Caspar looked content, Angel couldn't bring himself to feel happy. If the cannons had functioned perfectly and their capabilities been fully realized, then maybe the tragedy at the gate wouldn't have occurred.

No ifs or buts…

Still, it would have been possible to avoid that scene.

Being unable to improve the cannons or to confirm their results meant being left with nothing but frustration.

"You seem unhappy, but you should be proud."

"Easy for you to say…"

"They say the Survey Corps was being chased by ten Titans. Only one of 'em managed to get near Wall Maria."

"Ten?!"

"That means your cannons scattered the majority of them. I'd say that's good enough," Caspar grinned. "And you could say the Survey Corps returned safely 'cause they intercepted the Titans with those cannons, eh? I bet they feel safer, too."

"You're placing me on quite the pedestal, but did you call me in here to talk about cannons?"

"Just an aside. I wanted to talk to you about something else."

"I thought so. First the carrot, then the stick?"

As Angel smiled bitterly, the door to the chief's office opened.

"Did you call for me, chief?"

The unconcerned face that appeared belonged to Xenophon Harkimo, a workshop big shot in his mid-thirties known by his disheveled head of hair, stained work clothes, and metal-framed glasses. He was the former "master inventor" and Angel's senior at the workshop, though in its results-based world, Angel stood above him.

Not this guy.

Xenophon's body smelled faintly of chemicals, likely because of some sort of shady experiment he had just been conducting. He was probably concocting a new type of gunpowder. Xenophon's specialty was developing and manufacturing explosives, and the shells and gunpowder used in the cannons were Xenophon's handiwork.

Why's he here?

Angel glanced at Xenophon, who did not even show signs of returning a look.

He's probably thinking the same thing, though.

That, or he still held a grudge after his place as master inventor had been taken from him. In any case, the title was nothing more than a moniker applied by those around them. It wasn't as if Angel had stolen it from Xenophon.

"You've heard about the factory city, right?" Caspar suddenly said.

"The city the royal government is building in secret?" Xenophon looked pensive as he stroked the stubble on his chin.

Angel had heard the rumors, too. The town was like an open secret among the craftsmen, but he had never heard more than what Xenophon had just said. There may have been a gag order by the royal government, as he didn't even know where the city was being built.

"If it's a factory city, it must have something to do with us, huh?"

"Eventually, all workshops will move their operations there. The plan is to make it exactly what its name suggests. The facilities there will make what we have now pale in comparison, which should let us make new, ground-breaking equipment."

"I see. I bet we'd be able to process Iron Bamboo there, too," Xenophon mumbled in a chant-like monotone and pushed his glasses up.

"That may be an interesting material to work with, but there's supposed to be something even better in the factory city."

"Supposed to be? You don't have it with you?"

"No," Caspar quickly replied, then continued. "I couldn't have any ready for today, but I did get permission to go on-site. Go see it for yourself."

"When did they complete the city?!" Xenophon jumped at that bit, apparently interested.

"It won't be fully operational for a while, but taking a look couldn't hurt."

"We're the ones who're going to have to do the work. I don't see why we have to make the trip in secret."

"It's a dangerous world out there. You can never be too sure."

"Is that the only reason?"

"The only one."

"Can't you come up with a better one? Lie if you have to," Angel groaned, putting his hand to his forehead.

"The factory city'll serve a bigger purpose than you can even imagine. That's why we have to prepare for any unforeseen circumstances."

"Like Titans?"

"The Titans might be absolute monsters, but there's nothing to be scared of as long as you don't go outside, is there?"

"So you're saying we should be scared of humans." Xenophon nodded multiple times, as if in agreement. "Humans can be cunning. Like a certain someone," he said, glaring at Angel.

"Even our impregnable walls can't protect us from attacks that come from the inside."

"Ah, so it's a counterterrorism measure. Okay. You know what they say, nothing scarier than an armed nutcase," Angel said, glancing sideways at Xenophon.

"The factory city will be a practical armory. If anti-establishment forces captured it, our country itself could be overthrown."

"Like those weirdoes that have been worshipping the Titans recently."

"In any case, the details about the factory city are being kept a secret, even to those who will be involved, in order to protect it from idiots like that."

"But we're fine?"

"You're our two stars. It's not a problem."

"You're not sending me into some sort of trouble, are you…"

Angel had a bad and nearly certain feeling that trouble was exactly what he was going to get. Caspar was the one bringing this up, proof that a messy job was waiting.

"So, how do we get to the factory city?"

"You'll have navigators. Just follow them."

"Wouldn't a map suffice?"

"Slow to catch on, aren't you? They're obviously not letting you go alone."

"Why not?"

"Like I just mentioned, there are some dangerous people out there. The men with you are there to protect any secrets and to keep you safe."

"And they can shut our mouths, if the need arises?"

"That's the idea."

"Of all the times to agree with me…"

Caspar laughed heartily as Angel's shoulders sagged. "Anyway. Go see for yourselves. And if you can develop a new weapon while you're there, all the better!"

"You make it sound so easy."

"Well, I'm not the one doing the work."

Angel laughed bitterly.

***

"How are you going to use the Iron Bamboo?" Xenophon began speaking to Angel as soon as they left the chief's office. "Even for you, processing that stuff should be hard."

"Harvesting it must have been tough, too."

Simply pruning it ruined multiple knives, so cutting down a stem must have been nearly impossible. Before they could start thinking about how to use it, they first needed tools and facilities to process Iron Bamboo.

"Why don't we forget about processing it and just sell it to the Corps raw? It'd probably be way more useful to them than the blades they carry."

"Like a bamboo sword?" asked Xenophon.

"It'd affect our reputation as craftsmen, though."

"The situation might change once we're in the factory city."

Xenophon's eyes gleamed in apparent excitement. His breathing grew wild, and words were pouring from his mouth. "You're interested in the factory city, too, aren't you?"

"I *am* a craftsman, after all."

Angel's excitement was natural. Not only did he have Iron Bamboo, a new material, to work with, the factory city was about to become operational. He normally had a contentious relationship with Xenophon, but this was enough to put that aside for now. Xenophon may have been a thorn in his side, and it was true that they didn't get along, but the man was truly skilled as a craftsman. Angel could at least trust him on that point.

"Should we start by looking at ways to use it as a weapon?"

"Something that hard is just asking to be used as one."

"Very true."

"It may even be able to injure the Titans."

Unlike human skin, Titan skin was difficult to penetrate. Just as

Angel's short sword had no effect on the Iron Bamboo, blades could barely touch Titan skin. Even if they did injure a Titan, the monsters possessed extraordinary recuperative powers and healed within minutes. This was one of the reasons Titans were said to be unkillable.

But I don't know if I really buy that.

Unless they were using magic, healing a wound in moments was impossible.

That, or they truly are monsters…

Either way, Angel couldn't dispel his doubts until he saw the Titans for himself.

"It seems like Iron Bamboo leaves could be worth using, too."

"If we can even cook that goose."

"And that's going to be up to us."

"Let's at least try to come up with something better than bamboo swords." Angel looked to the sky. "Why don't we make it our homework for until we head to the factory city? We have such an interesting material on our hands."

Xenophon threw a hand up and walked off mumbling, "Development geek."

Angel chuckled, then began to amble, considering different ideas for the Iron Bamboo.

***

With the first cockcrow, the violet eastern sky gradually began to grow white, signaling that dawn had come. Before long, the morning sun would come out into view. The air outside was cold enough to make one's flesh and bones feel frozen over and to turn every breath steaming white. A cloak wasn't enough to stave off shivers.

"I understand that the factory city is a secret, but do we really have to leave this early in the morning?"

Angel stretched out as he yawned. He had been too excited to sleep, going the entire night without much rest. The shockingly cold air helped dispel some of his drowsiness, but it still took all his focus to keep from dozing off.

On the other hand, Xenophon, his companion, was the very image of excitement, though his eyes were bloodshot. Perhaps it was not so much that he, too, hadn't gotten enough sleep, but rather that he'd simply given up on getting any shut-eye at all.

"The city's construction may be an open secret, but I guess they can't just put it out in public."

"Do people already know about the factory city?" Corina remarked insouciantly. She had been allowed to come on the trip as Angel's assistant.

"No matter how much you try to control information, you can't sew people's mouths shut. The anti-establishment groups probably know about it, at least."

"Politicians might have leaked the information, too. It seems like something you could use as a bargaining chip."

"It's a money tree. People must be making all kinds of moves we don't know about."

"It's of no concern to craftsmen like us, though."

Angel shrugged his shoulders. Even if something political was happening within the royal government, it wasn't something he, Angel, could do anything about. He didn't have any interest in politics, either. A craftsman's job was to develop the best arms possible.

We're completely prepared. It's up to whatever ideas we have, now.

Their backpacks were full of all the tools needed to manufacture arms, and they had also brought Iron Bamboo with them as material to work with. They had somehow managed to prune the Iron Bamboo and cut it into one-meter-long pieces. It was the bare minimum of preparation, yet it had taken more labor and ruined tools to complete these minimal steps than to create one of the cannons now sitting on the Wall.

I can't come back with nothing better than a bamboo sword.

If that were to happen, it would mean more than just a scolding from Caspar. Then again, even if they did manage to create a revolutionary new weapon, whether it would be used or not would be up to how the government officials felt. The political situation would come into play, too. There was even the ridiculous yet real possibility that their creation would be passed on because it was too effective.

I bet it'd be inconvenient for some people if we started defeating Titans…

An external enemy was needed in order to maintain the walled cities. It went without saying that the Titans were being used by some as political leverage.

So in the end, we're still the ones on the short end of the stick.

As Angel sighed and scratched his head, he noticed Corina looking at him.

"Something wrong?"

"Your collar is twisted."

Corina reached out and fixed his turned collar.

"You should pay more attention to your appearance."

"Stop sounding like Maria…"

"I think she would be much stricter than I'm being."

Corina grinned, then nodded, satisfied with Angel's appearance.

"What a waste of a master inventor."

"Shut up," Angel scowled.

It seemed to be just moments before sunrise. The east sky was growing brighter.

"It looks like our ride is here," Corina said, pointing down the dim avenue. When Angel's eyes followed her gesture, he saw a wagon and four mounted soldiers approaching.

"Must be our famous navigators."

They knew that soldiers were supposed to be leading them to the factory city, but the security was so heavy it seemed as though the troops were there to guard VIPs.

"Were you waiting long?"

An unexpected man held the reins of the wagon on the driver's seat.

"Solm? When'd you quit your job to work as a coachman?"

"I'd consider it if the money was good, but I'm happy with where I am for the time being."

Solm stopped the coach in front of Angel and the others, then pointed at the cart.

"I can't make any guarantees about how comfortable the ride will be, but I promise you'll get there safely."

The cart had a canopy top, so it was protected from the elements, but it had no suspension, which meant they would be feeling every bump on the road. In other words, they were in for a rough ride.

"I should probably take something for travel sickness," Angel sighed as he threw his backpack into the cart.

***

Shiganshina District was connected to other towns by unpaved roads. Most building stones had been reserved for repairing and reinforcing Wall Maria and were not available for paving any roads. To begin with, the main mode of transportation was by horse, so it inconvenienced few people.

There were a number of major roads among the highways, and the artery that connected the Shiganshina and Trost Districts was vital to transportation and trade. Trost District was the town on the southern-most tip of Wall Rose, built in the same way as Shiganshina District. It would act as the front line of defense if Wall Maria were breached. For now, though, it was located well inside the Walls, so it was not as constantly aware of the Titans as Shiganshina District.

"Let me quickly explain today's itinerary," Solm announced as he drove the coach forward. "We'll start by heading toward Trost District. It'll take five or six hours. We'll get lunch once we arrive."

"If we have any appetite left, of course," Angel mumbled, fighting his nausea. It had only been thirty minutes since they left Shiganshina District, but he was on the verge of being bested by travel sickness. His inner ears seemed to be thrown for a loop, and his vision was shaking violently. He had done a good job of not vomiting, but there was no telling how much longer he could stand this. Xenophon and Corina were even sicker than Angel, and moans came from both of their green faces. Talking about lunch was no different from torture.

"Either way, we'll squeeze in a break in Trost District, then we'll head to the factory city."

"How long will it take?"

"A few hours, I suppose."

"Great…" Angel sighed deeply. "But why are you our navigator?"

"It's part of my job as your guard. It's not like I was assigned to just be your driver."

"I never thought the day would come when you'd be protecting me."

"Well, someone else was supposed to take command… Basically, I'm here in place of a team leader that died during the last expedition."

"A team leader? Do you mean Heath?"

"You know about him?"

"We never met, but a little."

The image of his flattened head and flying brains was still fresh in Angel's mind, but he had no intention of talking about it. The travel sickness already had him in an awful mood, and there was no need to make things even less pleasant.

In order to suppress his nausea, Angel somewhat forcefully changed the subject.

"By the way, have you decided when your wedding will be?"

"That's abrupt."

"You've been talking about it for a while, haven't you?"

"I have?"

"Hey, you better not play too many games with Maria. You'll make her cry."

"I know," Solm said flatly. "Have you heard the rumor that they might dissolve the Survey Corps?"

"When don't you hear that rumor?"

Solm responded to Angel's point with a bitter laugh. "The situation's a little different this time. It's honestly a critical moment for the Survey Corps."

"You seem popular enough with the townspeople, don't you?"

"The Survey Corps' job isn't to be popular." Solm shrugged, then added, "The political situation is changing."

"What do you mean?"

"I mean the conservative faction is starting to gain more power."

"Oh, the shut-ins?"

"The royal government isn't a monolith. The reformers and the conservatives are constantly fighting each other."

"And the conservatives have the momentum right now."

In other words, there were many inside the royal government who argued that humanity should give up on the land it lost to the Titans and live a modest existence inside the Walls. If the conservatives gained influence, it followed that the Survey Corps, who ventured outside the walls, was in danger of being dissolved. Furthermore, the Survey Corps had produced very few results since their inception. The conservatives would naturally try to make an example out of the Survey Corps, and the only way to counter them would be to produce results impressive enough to shut them up.

The factory city seems like it might end up taking a different role, too.

As there were rumors that a mint would be built in the factory city, the place would probably continue to be a secret, but it seemed likely that the city's scale would shrink as well.

"I bet we'd see a lot of changes if you could just bring back a Titan head."

"I'd like to if we could, but…"

"You can't kill the Titans?"

But as long as the Titans were organisms, they had to have weaknesses, and killing them had to be within the realm of possibility.

If I could just investigate the Titans, I'd be able to prove it.

Receiving permission to investigate them wasn't something he could expect, though. The situation would turn around completely if they discovered that the Titans could be killed. It would be an inconvenient state of affairs for those who feared change, especially the conservatives.

"As a member of the Survey Corps, I want to be able to have a legacy."

"So that's why you can't commit to getting married."

"That's why I'm expecting a lot from you."

"Me?"

"Once the factory city becomes operational, you should be able to produce new and unprecedented weapons. The facilities to make them don't exist anywhere else."

"I don't want you getting your hopes up too much."

Solm and Maria's futures, in particular, were too heavy a burden to bear. All Angel could do was develop arms and provide them to soldiers. It was Solm's job to use those and leave a legacy.

New weapons, huh.

Angel took the Iron Bamboo in his hand and fell into thought.

While he had yet to be visited by any inspirations, he had a groundless faith that the Iron Bamboo would lead to some sort of amazing invention. That proved its hidden potential.

"But what I need right now…" Angel said as he lied down, "is some sleep." He braced to fight the nausea assaulting him.

***

The temperature dropped as soon as they entered the other side of Wall Rose. The elevation there was much higher than the area around Wall Maria. The closer to Wall Sheena one got, the higher the elevation became, and the area beyond Wall Sheena was a thousand feet in altitude. While it depended on the season, the temperature was as much as five degrees colder.

As the coach drew closer to Wall Sheena, it left the artery and entered a side road, doggedly making its way north. Even off the artery, they were heading toward Wall Sheena.

"Are we still far from the factory city?" Corina faintly let out, raising her hand. While her face was still pale, it wasn't the sickened green it'd been immediately after departing. Her body must have been adjusting to the swaying carriage. The same could be said for Angel and Xenophon, but the main reason their travel sickness had improved was that the carriage was now moving slower. This, of course, had been by request, and it meant they were running far behind schedule.

Five hours had passed since they left Trost District, but they had yet to see a single building that suggested the factory city's presence. Even if they had wanted to check the area, the sun had already completely set. The two soldiers who led the convoy lit the forest path with torches, but these only provided an unreliable light that outlined their surroundings. All that could be made out were coniferous trees: cypress, pine, and cedar. They were far from towns and villages, and there was zero pedestrian traffic on their path.

"We'll get there in two hours if we hurry. But at this pace, it'll take double that."

Solm skillfully maneuvered the reins as he forged ahead on the narrow path that now nearly resembled an animal trail.

"So we either put up with nausea or face the alternative. What a pair of crummy options," Xenophon said with a disgusted face.

Angel felt no different. "I'd rather not vomit myself dry…"

"Then you'll just have to be patient," Solm answered bluntly. He added, "We can't go fast when it's this dark out. I doubt we'll be able to tour the factory city, either. Going at this speed is the best option, don't you think?"

Solm's proposal was convincing enough to silence the complainers.

"In that case, I trust myself to our coachman. I'm getting some sleep."

Right as Angel made to roll back down, a shot rang out and the horses neighed. The coach came to a sudden stop, and Angel and the other passengers fell forward on the cart while their stacked luggage tumbled off.

"What happened?" Angel, regaining his posture, called out towards the driver's seat and Solm.

"Keep your head down. You'll get yourself shot."

Solm grabbed the flare gun on his hip, pointed it above his head, and pulled the trigger. The released signal shot straight up into the air and was swallowed by the darkness.

For a moment, they were surrounded by silence.

Then, the White Star exploded in the sky above with a flash of light that filled their dark world.

Huh? What just happened?!

Angel tried to get a glance of what was in front of the wagon, staying as low as he could.

That's…

He was able to see the bodies of two cavalrymen on the ground around ten meters ahead of him. They were the carriage's front guards. Both of their chests were stained red, and while it was possible they were still alive, they showed no signs of moving. There appeared to have been no struggle, suggesting an ambush.

"I think they're dead," submitted Xenophon.

"Yeah," Angel replied, his face stiff. He was sad to see them go, but he didn't have the luxury to be mourning their deaths. For all he knew, he was only moments away from joining them. Inevitably he was growing tense.

"Look. Someone's there."

Xenophon pointed ahead with his chin. Angel followed the gesture to see a group of nearly a dozen mounted figures around fifty meters ahead of the two bodies.

"Are those…enemies?"

They could have been bandits, or perhaps they were anti-establishment forces. Clearly they were not some trade caravan. As if to drive the point home, they all held short swords, while a number of them also had guns, probably the ones that did the soldiers in.

"Are we going to be all right?" Corina seemed uneasy as she leaned in close to Angel with a worried expression.

I want to tell her not to be scared, but…

Angel felt worried about the situation, too. Though he was hardly in any mental state to say something to comfort her, he forced a smile and placed a hand on Corina's head.

"Just leave this to the professionals. It'll work out."

"We *are* hugely outnumbered, though," Xenophon pointed out the harsh reality, then darted around gathering thumb-sized vials that had been scattered across the cart.

"What are you doing, at a time like this?"

"Precisely because it's a time like this," Xenophon said with a straight face, but Angel could not figure out his intention.

He didn't know what was inside the vials, nor did he care to know, but it had to be some sort of chemicals harmful to humans.

"Isn't there anyone stationed around here that can help us?" Angel called to Solm.

"The signal flare should have caught their eye, but this is going to be all over by the time they get here."

"So we can't count on any backup…"

In other words, they had to gird themselves and handle this on their own. Still, it wasn't easy to adopt such a mindset, especially in a milieu as unfamiliar as combat.

"Humans are scarier than Titans. Just like I told you, right?"

Carefully cradling the vials, Xenophon looked outside from near the driver's seat.

"I think they're anti-establishment forces. Regular citizens don't carry guns."

"It might be those Titan lovers, no?"

"If you're going to worship the Titans, then you'd be in Shiganshina District. I don't see why they'd be this far in the interior."

"There's only one thing they want. To—"

"Enough," Solm said, interrupting and putting an end to Angel and Xenophon's conversation.

"We're going to force our way through! Get low, it's going to get rough!!"

As soon as Solm yelled, he whipped the horse. It let out a powerful neigh and rushed the carriage forward.

This is awful…

The carriage shook in every direction as if an earthquake had just struck. While they had been told to get down, they wouldn't have been able to stay upright had they wished to. They'd naturally taken cover on the floor, but Corina's petite body bobbed up and down together with the shaking cart.

Just as Angel caught Corina, who was bouncing like a ball, more shots sounded and a number of them tore holes in the canopy.

At this rate we'll all be turned into beehives.

They had to do something soon but were helpless to act from inside the wagon. The coach sped down the wooded path as if it were charging, but their enemies were doing the same. While the canopy made it difficult to get an accurate grasp of the situation, the ferocious, beastly cries and galloping were gaining on them like a wave.

Moments later, the battle began. It seemed to have turned into a melee, as they could keenly tell that both sides were jostling and shoving one another.

"We're in a bad spot."

"What's going to happen to us…"

The shrill, metallic sound of clashing blades could be heard from all around, and with them came scream after scream. It instinctively made them want to cover their ears, but they were too busy coping with the shaking cart.

Suddenly, something tore through the canopy. Wind rushed in through the tear, flipped the canopy, then violently stripped it off the wagon. The moment their field of vision opened up, their situation became clear. The carriage was surrounded by enemies carrying short swords, and there was no visible escape path.

What about our guards? Where are our allies?!

Angel scanned the area for help. The guards were fighting hard to repel the enemy but were swamped.

A menacing blade closed in on Angel.

"Aah…"

The murderous intent he could see deep within his foe's eyes made Angel tremble the moment he saw them. While he may have encountered malice from time to time during his everyday life, it was the first time he had ever looked into eyes ready to kill. But as Angel cowered, the assailant mercilessly swung his short sword down toward him.

"A-Ack!"

Letting out a pathetic cry, Angel bent his body backward as far as it would go. The glinting blade passed through the air before him. If he had swayed even a moment later, his head would surely have been split open.

"I was under the impression that we'd been promised safety," Xenophon objected sarcastically, tossing one of the vials he held toward a foe. The man swiftly avoided it, but before it could hit the ground, the vial exploded with a sound like a firecracker, emitting what looked like bolts of lightning. It was not enough to draw blood, a modest fireworks that merely burnt anyone who came in direct contact, but it did have its element of surprise. One rider's horse bucked, tossing him to the ground.

"You brought stun grenades?"

"Of course not. I just put those together a minute ago."

"You made them?!"

"Precisely at a time like this, didn't I tell you?" Xenophon shot back as he opened his vials and began mixing the chemicals inside. Now that the canopy had been lost, though, the wind conspired with the rough ride to make his job nearly impossible. The enemies they needed to defeat loomed right in front of them too, hardly a suitable environment for such work. Unsurprisingly, the chemicals inside the vials were swept away before Xenophon could mix them.

With that option gone, Xenophon grabbed a wrench, but it made for a rather skimpy argument. Indeed, the tool flew into the air after just one incoming strike. Left unarmed, Xenophon emitted a ridiculous scream.

A weapon... I need a weapon...

It was a bad joke; a professional weaponsmith, even capable of making cannons, unarmed. It wasn't beyond Angel, as it hadn't been for Xenophon, to combine some of the scattered materials to create armaments, but the situation was just too unfriendly for that. He needed a weapon, but it was no use if it couldn't be wielded right away.

No other choice...

It would only be a matter of time before they were killed unless they did something. As Angel put his hand to the floor in order to pick himself up and prepare for the enemy's attacks, he felt something at his fingertips. They had brought the steel rod-like object with them as material.

"Iron Bamboo…"

The moment he took it in his hands, Angel had a flash of inspiration.

If I used this…

While the Iron Bamboo was barely-prepped raw material, it was still harder than any weapon Angel had ever come across. It was easy to tell from its extraordinary hardness that it could be used on its own as a weapon. Angel handed one to Xenophon.

"It's just a bamboo sword, but you can use this, can't you?"

"So a mere pruning does processing make."

As soon as Xenophon took the Iron Bamboo, he began swinging it around. His bent posture made his lack of experience clear for all to see, but unlike with his wrench, he was not going to be disarmed the next time he clashed weapons.

"Now we are talking! This will do!!"

"Yeah, seems like it."

Angel, too, swung the Iron Bamboo, keeping up. He had no knowledge of quarterstaff fighting and it was his first battle, but the pole's meter-long length offered an advantage. Though a blade of the same length would be heavy and unwieldy, the Iron Bamboo was exceedingly light, and their enemies were mounted, too. Unlike Angel, who could use both arms, they needed to keep one hand on the reins. While he may have never learned how to, he'd still be able to put up a fight.

Angel raised the Iron Bamboo above his head, then made a roughly diagonal slash. Its tip landed squarely on an enemy's shoulder, pulverizing bone. The man somersaulted off of his horse.

The strike signaled the beginning of the counteroffensive. Their enemies faltered, and the soldiers used the opportunity to rush straight into them. The tide of the battle turned in moments as they struck down one foe after the other.

"Giddyap!"

The carriage accelerated as Solm whipped his horse. In the distance, they could see what looked like a signal flare from incoming backup.

CHAPTER TWO

Having survived the assault by anti-establishment forces, Angel and the others finally made it to the factory city. They were a few hours later than originally scheduled; not so late that a new day had already come, but it certainly wasn't the best time of day to be checking out the place. It was half-built and spottily lit by lanterns that dotted it like fireflies. Covered in darkness, the city was no place for a stroll let alone a tour.

No doubt because they were unable to see it in its entirety, they had little to no thoughts on the factory city. While Angel surely would have voiced an impression had it been daytime, all he felt was a sense of relief at arriving alive. His mind was completely devoid of any interest in the city's appearance or the factories' equipment. Perhaps any eagerness he once held had fallen by the roadside during their wild carriage ride.

In any case, they required a place where they could sleep in peace. They were so totally exhausted that they were ready to say it was the only thing they needed, and in fact, they headed straight for their lodgings.

Still, there was one thing that Angel took strong notice of. A sound. To be precise, the sound of water. It wasn't the sound of rain, nor a murmuring stream. Perhaps there was a waterfall nearby. He could vividly imagine huge amounts of water thunderously flowing and falling.

There was certainly a plentiful amount of it involved as the roar was loud enough to hear inside their rooms. It must have been one of the sources providing Shiganshina District with its water. The realization ought to have been sublime, but sadly, for the time being Angel only heard a lullaby that coaxed him to sleep.

***

The first floor of the lodging facility was a lounge that also served as the cafeteria. The room could fit as many as a hundred people and was bustling with activity. Over half of the people there were, like Angel, craftsmen. They congregated in their own groups and spoke excitedly about whatever topics interested them.

A number of similar installations had been built in the factory city, and the one that Angel and the others stayed at was for visitors. As it was built on the assumption that its inhabitants would be there for short, roughly one-week stays, the facilities were incredibly plain. The rooms had simple interiors, with little more than the beds taking their pride of place.

The problem was that while they were in a cafeteria, they could not find anyone in charge of meals. Instead, they found boxes full of canned foods stacked in tall piles.

"Is canned food really the best way to start the day?" Angel sighed as he looked at the set lined up on his table.

It's not like I was expecting local specialties, but this is a little extreme...

While he was not going to request a royal feast, he had at least hoped for a warm meal, especially after going hungry the day before thanks to a long battle with nausea.

"They're letting us eat for free, so I don't know if it's really our place to be picky..." Corina chastised him as she used a can opener to unceremoniously pop the cans.

So we have meat, beans, fish, and dried fruit.

Disregarding the fact that everything was canned, they had a reasonably large selection. These food supplies must have come from an emergency stockpile.

I wonder about the expiration date...

As they smelled fine, they probably wouldn't cause any upset stomachs. As far as taste, though, they seemed little more than edible.

"Have you ever had field rations before? These are delicious in comparison." Solm pried the top of a can off with a knife and stabbed into a piece of dried meat. "They were made so that you could eat them on a horse, so not only do they taste miserable, they're hard as rocks."

As Solm voiced his discontent, Xenophon was up to something with his vials. "You only need to do a bit of work," he opined, "to make canned food taste good."

"What're you doing?"

"It's called cooking," Xenophon replied casually as he began mixing chemicals on top of his plate.

"Nothing's going to explode, right?"

"Do you really think I'd mess up like that?"

Xenophon opened the top to a vial and poured the liquid inside over the powders he had combined on his plate. Then, as if by magic, a bluish-white flame appeared.

"In place of solid fuel. How about the rest of you?"

Xenophon grinned as he began broiling his meat in the flame.

"I'll pass." Angel may have wanted a warm meal, but he had no interest in using the flame. If there were any deadly poisons among Xenophon's chemicals, he would have to deal with a lot more than a stomach ache.

"These are the same chemicals that go into signal flares. Change the ingredients and you'll get a Red Star, a Green Star, or a Yellow Star. Of course, White Stars emit the most light, so the rest are basically smoke signals."

Sticking some lightly-salted cooked beans in his mouth, Angel asked Solm, "Speaking of White Stars, what happened to those guys from last night?"

"Those guys? We handed them off to the Military Police Brigade. They're almost certainly members of the anti-establishment forces."

"Still, I didn't think we'd be attacked... What's in it for them?"

"Identifying the factory city's location. That, or kidnapping a craftsman." Solm chuckled bitterly then continued, "Anyway, as long as this place is full of soldiers, it won't fall into enemy hands."

"You're confident."

"Of course I am."

"You know, they say that the majority of the members of the anti-establishment forces are people from the countryside," Xenophon noted. "There are numerous tired hamlets in this country that we don't even put on maps. The people there would see these as luxuries," he said, pointing to a can.

"So we should feel blessed."

"Especially because Shiganshina District gets preferential tax treatment. It seems likely that they'd feel it's unfair."

While there had to be more reasons behind the anti-establishment forces' existence, it was true that hunger impoverished the heart and the body. One could say that the groups were amalgamations of accumulated grievances.

"We'll let the Military Police Brigade deal with them, but meanwhile you seem awfully savvy about them. Possibly some sort of suspicious relationship."

Angel glanced at Xenophon.

"Could you please stop with the blatantly false accusations?"

"Oh? Don't you think they'll start confessing to all kinds of crimes, real or not, after a few days in the care of the Military Police Brigade?"

"Why should anyone confess to something he didn't do?" Xenophon sighed in disgust.

**

The factory city far surpassed Angel's expectations. While he had thought it would be no larger than a village, it was as expansive as Shiganshina District, and they eventually expected 50,000 people to live there. In addition to residential quarters where craftsmen and their families would live, there were also commercial facilities and amusement quarters to take care of their daily needs. The factories there, it went without saying, were fully equipped. The city's functions would clearly outstrip Shiganshina District's once finished, but the majority of the structures were still under construction. Relocating the workshop was not yet an urgent matter.

"What a view, though."

Angel stared out at the grand waterfall located at the northern end of the city and the soaring mountains that stood behind it. The gushing cascade spanned five hundred meters across, with a drop of a hundred. While its unrestrained force reminded one of a flash flood, the water-power it generated was central to the factory city. The potential it offered was the reason behind the city's location.

The waterfall was not the only part of the factory city that drew one's eye. In the center of the city loomed a giant building that could easily be called a landmark.

"So that's the steel mill. Jeez…"

The blast furnace, the mill's symbol, was over fifty meters tall and would surely come to represent the city. It consumed the majority of the energy produced by the waterfall. The water itself would be used to cool equipment and pig iron. Though they could smelt ore into pig iron at the workshop, the scale of the factory city's facilities was on a completely different level.

Corina stared up at the gigantic blast furnace with a look of wonder in her eyes. "Just look at how much bigger it is."

"It looks ten times larger than the one we have."

"Which means it can produce ten times as much, too."

"I bet it would have been a lot easier to meet the fulfillment if I could've used this thing for the cannons."

The factory city's blast furnace would allow them to handle large-scale orders with little to no problem. They'd be under less stress, which would let them focus on their work.

Looks like centralization can offer a lot of benefits.

They would be able to say goodbye to the days of complaining about a lack of time, capacity, and all the other things that they were short on.

"It looks like they've finished lighting it. The coal's burning bright red."

Through the peephole down to the bottom of the furnace, they could see its copper-red fuel emitting massive amounts of heat.

"That's not coal, it's coke."

"Coke?"

"It's a purer fuel made by baking coal. It's vital to making pig iron because of the high amount of heat it generates."

"We use coal at our workshop," Angel snickered.

Solm spoke up. "So, think you can come up with any ideas?"

"The furnace is good, and if we use the converter, we should probably be able to refine some new alloys."

Whether that would lead to any ideas for new arms was a different question.

"That reminds me. Wasn't there some material here that's even more interesting than the Iron Bamboo?"

"You mean the Iceburst Stone?"

"Ice...what?"

"Iceburst Stone. Has the chief not told you anything?"

"Not a thing." Angel shrugged and let out a sigh.

"Some sort of rare metal, judging by the name?"

"He really hasn't told you anything, has he?"

"Probably too much of a pain to explain."

There was no way of knowing what Caspar was thinking at that moment, but he may have been imagining and guffawing at Angel's confused expression.

Corina's eyes seemed to be sparkling with an interest in this new material. "So what are these Ice-Burstones like?"

"How about we finish with the steel mill for now and move to the mining site?"

Angel and Corina agreed to Solm's proposal, but Xenophon seemed to have something else on his mind and kept staring at the blast furnace with a pensive look.

"I'm going to stay behind."

"You don't want to see the Iceburst Stone?"

"Yes. I'll leave that to you. I want to do a little experiment here."

They couldn't tell what Xenophon had in mind, but he wore the expression of a child who had just come up with a devious prank.

I'm pretty sure I know what he wants to do, anyway. There was only one experiment Angel could think of that used a blast furnace. *I wonder what he'll make with the Iron Bamboo.*

Angel wouldn't have minded sticking around to witness an Iron

Bamboo's moment of rebirth but didn't care to spoil Xenophon's fun. The man's report on the results would do. While Angel had a lingering interest in the Iron Bamboo, his attention was quickly turning toward the Iceburst Stone.

***

The factory city's existence was so thoroughly concealed because it was one of a kind. Though there were any number of waterfalls throughout the country, this was the only location with such a grand cascade. If it were to fall into the enemies' hands, the country itself could be overthrown. The waterpower produced by the falls was immense and inexhaustible, and they had yet to find a comparable source of energy. As there were also plans to build a mint in the factory city, the royal government was surely keeping a special eye on it. Its eventual importance in politics, too, was certain.

This was reason enough to hide the existence of the factory city, but there was even more hidden beneath the surface.

"So next we're going to go behind the scenes?"

Angel stared at the soaring cliffs in front of him. On first glance, there was nothing more to the location on the northern edge of town than the falls. That was not the only thing there, though, and Solm had taken them to a precipitous cliff to the side. What he wanted to show them was not its rock face but the cave whose mouth gaped there.

Corina stared inside from the entrance. "It looks pretty big. How far does it stretch?"

"We don't know for sure. One thing we do know is that it's full of detours, so if you get lost in there, you're not coming out alive."

"Perfect conditions to turn you into grave wax. Maybe we can use some bodies in place of our torches."

"I'm not a fan of candles and mummies…" objected Corina.

"We have the fruits of civilization available to us, so we won't have to defile any corpses." Solm raised his lantern, removed its glass chimney, and lit the wick.

61

"How long will the fuel last for?"

"Half a day. We only need thirty minutes if we're just going to see Iceburst Stone."

"So we should be able to leave before getting ourselves lost."

"Isn't there a chance that you'll become enraptured with the material?"

"I won't rule out the possibility."

No craftsman alive could resist the allure of a new material to work with, hence Solm's fear.

"I know we didn't have any samples at the workshop, but are these Ice-Burstones that rare?"

"No, there are piles of them."

"In that case, couldn't you at least have brought one out for us?"

"You'll understand once you touch one," Solm stated firmly and headed in, lantern in hand.

Angel and Corina followed behind.

***

The cave was biting cold. It was already at a high enough altitude to be chilly on the outside, but inside, it was like an ice house. The temperature was near freezing, so protection against it was indispensable for anyone going in for a significant period of time. In other words, the almost completely unprepared party would not be able to stay inside the cave as they were even if they wanted to.

The cave's footing was poor and slippery, possibly from frozen water that had seeped out from under the ground. It was like walking on frozen pavement, but with the ceilings and walls frozen as well, the place was more like a cavern of ice. The world around them took in the light from the lantern and randomly scattered it about, creating a fairly unreal scene. The cave led underground, broadening before them as they went deeper. There were side paths, too, giving a sense of reality to Solm's earlier warning about getting lost.

"There it is."

Solm stopped and raised his lantern.

"This is incredible."

In front of them was a gigantic space and an underground lake. It was so large that the lantern couldn't light the entire thing, but they could tell that the area in front of them was wide open.

"This used to be what you'd call a caldera. At least, that's what some important professor told me."

"So we're looking at a caldera lake. I see."

"But that water seems a little…" Corina walked to the edge of the lake, stooped, and touched its surface. "It's frozen solid."

"It might look like water, but that's not ice."

"It's not?" Following Corina's lead, Angel touched the lake. His eyes and his fingers told him it was ice. "This has to be ice."

"Nope."

Solm unsheathed the short sword he carried on his hip and used it to stab the surface of the lake. The ice broke apart easily, and Solm picked up a fragment the size of the tip of his thumb.

"It's Iceburst Stone."

"This?" Angel stared at the piece Solm held. "Are you sure it's not just a regular pebble?" That was indeed his only impression of it.

"Let me show you something neat."

Putting the lantern on the ground and removing its chimney, Solm put the Iceburst Stone on the tip of his blade and moved it toward the flame. It ignited into a quiet, bluish-white flame.

"That's…"

"The ice is burning!" Corina's eyes fluttered.

"It's too complicated for me to understand the details, but it's apparently made of gases that leak out from underground. Apparently there's an enormous amount of Iceburst Stone just sitting down here."

"Like a mountain full of treasure."

"Now I see why you didn't have a sample."

It made sense that Caspar had told them to see it for themselves. It was far more intuitive than having some gas sprayed in front of their faces.

"Have they started mining it yet?"

"It was just discovered. They haven't established how to extract or store the gas."

"And that's where we come in!" Corina flexed her thin arms.

"Something that uses gas, huh..."

Ideas for many boilerplate weapons passed through Angel's mind. A gas gun, a flamethrower, bombs...

If they're powerful enough, then maybe.

But even cannonballs couldn't hurt the monsters they were facing. Small arms were likely to be about as effective as a peashooter. In the worst case, they would just stir and anger the Titans.

If the Titans have emotions, of course.

Whatever the case, it was clear that they needed to produce a brand-new piece of equipment.

A flamethrower might be good.

While Titan skin repelled blades, perhaps it could be weakened with fire.

No, that wouldn't work...

A flamethrower with overwhelming firepower that could instantly roast a Titan and turn it to dust, sure. But realistically speaking, they'd need to inflict more than a few burns. Building gas lamps would be more beneficial to society.

Angel scowled and groaned.

"See, didn't I tell you?"

The voice jumped into Angel's ear, abruptly stopping his train of thought.

"What are you talking about?"

"About your being a development geek."

"I didn't expect you to actually get this into it," Corina chimed in.

"Well, excuse me for being a geek."

As Angel huffed, he stared at an Iceburst Stone fragment lying on the ground.

"Can you think of a use for it?" asked Solm.

"This one begs for some unique thinking unlike the Iron Bamboo."

"Trial and error will give us more interesting results in the end," observed Corina.

"I hope so."

Angel rolled the Iceburst Stone on the palm of his hand.

"What do you want to do? Go back for now?"

"Yes, let's. We can't do anything empty-handed like this, anyway."

Corina rubbed her arms around her shaking body. "We should prepare some cold-weather gear next time."

"Can we bring this stuff outside?"

"No, unfortunately."

"Seriously? Does some bigwig have a monopoly on it?"

"That's not what I mean. If you tried to bring it outside, then—boom!" Solm said with an exaggerated clap.

"It'll explode?!" exclaimed Corina.

"It expands and explodes at room temperature. That's why it's called Iceburst Stone."

"So we need some special way to extract the gas."

These properties seemed to be why the Iceburst Stone had yet to be mined, despite its high potential utility.

"Let's just go back for now. I can't start on anything without my tools," Angel said, tossing the Iceburst Stone fragment.

***

The amount of gas that could be extracted from Iceburst Stone was even greater than imagined. When vaporized, its volume expanded by as much as two hundred times. Finding the right use for it could mean dramatic changes in everyday life. If they could just prepare cylinders for transporting the gas, they'd be able to use it immediately.

"The problem is what to trap it in."

Angel fell deep into thought as he stared at an Iceburst Stone fragment. Considering its rate of expansion, any gas cylinder they used would need to be strong. While they could avoid the risk of explosion if they put less in each cylinder, it wouldn't be efficient.

"We'll need to design a cylinder…"

"That's a good idea, but could we have something to eat first?" Corina opened the can she brought from the lodging facilities, ignited an Iceburst Stone, and used the fire to warm her food.

"I see. Yet another way to use these stones."

"A warm meal enriches the heart."

"If they'd only also lead to flashes of inspiration." Angel grimaced, looking down at the now-steaming can.

It was full of the same unappetizing cooked beans that they'd had for breakfast. But now, possibly because of his chilled body, they looked oddly delicious. The steam wafting through the air might have been causing him to have visions.

"Maybe my problem is that I'm thinking about how to use the Iceburst Stone as a weapon."

"The Iron Bamboo seems more suited for that."

"I'm looking forward to seeing how Xenophon cooks that ingredient, but in all likelihood, he's going to make a short sword."

"Something to replace the standard equipment soldiers receive."

"It's light and hard. Couldn't ask for more."

The Iron Bamboo had proved its effectiveness during their skirmish with the anti-establishment forces.

"May I ask a question?" Corina said, raising her hand. She closely watched Angel's expression and ventured, "Why did you choose to become a craftsman?"

"That's an odd question."

"Well, it's not an easy job, and…"

"And the pay is bad?" Angel finished with a wry laugh. "If you're going to go demand better pay, I'll be in there with you."

"Ah, no, not like that. But I suppose higher pay would be nice," Corina admitted.

"I became a craftsman because of a promise I made when I was a child."

"A promise?"

"Yes, one that I made with Solm and Maria."

For as long as Angel could remember, he had been without a single relative. He had no idea who his parents were. He didn't know their names, so whether they were alive was a mystery to him, too. It was the same for any blood relations. The person who named him was the director of his orphanage. While it may have looked like an unfortunate situation to others, it was the only one he knew, and he never felt particularly lonely. In fact, he was more given to thinking about all that business now, after having grown up, than back then. Still, he knew nothing about his parents, even what they looked like, so he had no interest in learning more about them. Even if they were alive, they would be nothing more than strangers connected to him by blood, and any meeting would just be awkward. The parents who raised him outweighed the ones that had him.

It was thanks to the good environment he had, for an orphan, that Angel could grow up sound without any chip on his shoulder. One could even say that he had a fortunate childhood, as he never had to worry about basic necessities and even had a parent figure. The friends with whom he spent his days played an especially large role in his life, and Solm and Maria, who were close to his age, were like siblings to him. Each of their positions was clear. The solidly-built Solm was like the older brother, the firm and level-headed Maria was the older sister, and Angel was the troublesome little brother.

"Solm said something to me when we were kids. He asked me what I thought was happening beyond the Walls."

"So Mr. Hume had an interest in the Survey Corps even as a child?"

"I don't know if it was interest. He saw them more as a means. It's the only way to go out there, for the time being."

"Is the Survey Corps the kind of organization you can just decide to join because you want to?"

"I don't know. Getting in can't be easy, though."

"He must have had a strong will."

"Well, his body was pretty strong, too." Angel chuckled. "Things got crazy once he started saying he wanted to join the Survey Corps. Maria was completely against it."

"Of course she'd be. He could die, after all."

"Maria tried hard to dissuade him, but Solm's just too stubborn and wouldn't give in. That's why I decided to make Solm's dream come true."

"Didn't that make Miss Carlstedt furious?"

"Yeah, she was mad. But getting mad wouldn't change how Solm felt, would it? In that case, I needed to do what I could to make sure Solm came home alive and well."

"And that was to become a craftsman." Corina clapped her hands together in understanding.

"The survival rate for expeditions would rise if they only had a way to defeat the Titans."

"And that would cause Miss Carlstedt to stop worrying, too."

"It'd kill two birds with one stone."

"So Miss Carlstedt joined the Garrison to guard where Mr. Hume would be returning?"

Angel nodded at Corina's question. "That's pretty much it."

"It's really nice that you have that."

Starting to feel embarrassed by his own stories, Angel quickly tried to change the subject. "Anyway, back to the issue at hand."

"Looking at the Iceburst Stone, I started to think." Corina pointed at the Iceburst Stone as it burned a pale blue. "While it seems to have a solid shape, in reality, it doesn't."

"So it's a good fuel source but can't be used as a weapon?"

"It can be used as a power source, though."

"Like for a heater?"

"It might be nice to have one," Corina laughed, then continued. "The gas from it could be used to power something, just as the factory city uses waterpower."

"The question is, what's that something?" Angel laughed helplessly.

"For example, if you had some sort of equipment that allowed you to fight on even ground with a Titan, the gas could be used to power it."

"Equipment that allows you to fight on even ground with a Titan?"

"Hypothetically speaking."

"Okay, then. Hypothetically, what's needed for humans to fight evenly with Titans?"

"Um… What do Titans look like?!"

"Just imagine that they're gigantic humans."

Corina responded with a groan.

"It's a guess, but I think the Titans are about five or six meters tall."

"You've never seen one, have you?"

"I may not have ever seen one, but I've heard their footsteps."

Angel had had the opportunity at the Survey Corps' return parade the other day.

They're incredibly large, I know that much.

That much had been clear from the slight tremor in the ground.

"So visually speaking, the difference between humans and Titans is our sizes…" Corina continued, mumbling, her brow furrowed in thought. She seemed to be ordering her thoughts by speaking them aloud. "Whoever has the high ground in a battle is at an advantage, correct?"

"You hear that said often."

"The same logic might apply to the Titans."

"So it's like the Titans are attacking from high above."

"That seems to put humans in a bad spot."

To the Titans, humans must seem like nothing more than puppies playing underfoot. "If there was some sort of device to make up for that, then humans could fight against the Titans, huh?"

"Yes."

"I'm starting to get the idea."

"In other words, we just need to create something that improves a disadvantageous situation."

"Easier said than done."

"Don't worry about it." Perhaps having an idea in mind, Corina slapped her chest.

"You seem confident."

"I'm not the one who has to come up with it."

"Ugh, that sounds like something the old man would say…" Angel smiled bitterly as he scratched his head.

"Was I of any help?"

"Yeah. You've got talent in more ways than one."

"I'll take that as a compliment."

Corina gave a satisfied smile.

***

That night, Angel and Xenophon reported their results to one another over dinner.

"And that about does it as far as Iceburst Stone."

Having gone on about its possible uses and potential, Angel put a portable gas stove on the table.

"So this is what I tried making. It was originally Corina's idea, though."

"This is the fuel." Corina brought out a can and placed it inside the stove.

"It's cold inside the cave, right? Well, warm food tastes great in a cold place," Angel said, igniting the stove.

"The stove is fueled by Iceburst Stone. All we did was put some in an open can and weld it shut."

"We'll need specialized cylinders to transport it in large quantities."

"Looks like my chemicals are going to be put out to pasture," Xenophon lamented, stroking his beard.

"Not like they were doing much for us in the first place…"

Angel sighed and put a can of food on top of the stove.

"So, what'd you end up finding?" Solm asked.

Xenophon placed a hammer on the table. "It requires a fair bit of equipment to process metal extracted from Iron Bamboo. Jumping straight to making weapons was too much of a stretch."

"Thus the hammer. Makes sense."

The hammer seemed unremarkable, but it was shockingly light. Its weight meant that any able-bodied man or woman would be able to handle it easily.

That's Iron Bamboo for you.

While Angel didn't know how it felt in use, he imagined that it was suitably hard.

"Using this to forge the extracted metal, we should be able to come up with some fantastic weapons."

"I'm sure it won't be easy, but hone away."

It wasn't hard to imagine how difficult the work ahead of him would be, considering how hard the Iron Bamboo was.

"Oh, yes. I also made this." Xenophon brought out something that looked like the skeleton of a small fish.

"Trash?"

"My goodness. I resent that."

"What is it, then?"

"Still haven't noticed?" Xenophon grinned triumphantly. "This is an Iron Bamboo leaf."

"Iron Bamboo?!" Looking at it closer, Angel could tell that what looked like a skeleton was actually the veins of a leaf.

"You can dissolve the leaf to leave only the fibers behind. It just requires a little bit of temperature adjustment."

Corina pinched the Iron Bamboo leaf with her fingertips. "Are you going to make combat uniforms out of this?"

"I don't know anything about sewing, unfortunately. I'll keep it in mind, though."

"Only our first day, and we already have quite a few ideas. That's why they call you the workshop's two stars."

Solm sounded honestly impressed, but the true test of their abilities as craftsmen still lay ahead.

"The old man back home won't be happy with ideas alone. He's not so kind."

If a product cost too much, it wouldn't see real-world use, no matter how fine its performance. If its design was too complicated, it wasn't cut out for mass production. Creating a prototype was only the beginning. A craftsman truly showed his skill during the trial and error that followed.

"Well, we can't go home empty-handed. Might as well give it our best."

Angel looked at the can and reached out for the beans that danced inside.

***

Closing the gap with the Titans. Angel had decided that this was the short cut to contending with them. He was now trying to create a piece of equipment that would fill in one of those gaps: height. Even the physically blessed soldiers in the Survey Corps were like infants next to the Titans. The Survey Corps had no choice but to fight at their feet, and in the worst case, were simply flattened. But if Angel's equipment saw field use, then the soldiers could fight eye-to-eye with the Titans. It was likely to lead to a complete overhaul of tactics, too.

While there were some barriers that no amount of technology could overcome, the Survey Corps could cope by changing their approach. For example, it was impossible to use machines to imitate the Titans' recuperative abilities, but creating a weapon powerful enough to annul the disadvantage would have the same effect. Not knowing about the Titans' behavior was unfortunate, but if the Survey Corps obtained results, the situation would have to change.

As Angel imagined what the Titans looked like, he began to see the outlines of the Equipment.

***

There were a number of technical hurdles that Angel had to overcome to develop the Equipment. As an entirely novel invention, there was nothing he could use as reference. All of the parts were hand-made, one-of-a-kind items, requiring time and effort and difficult to fine-tune. He faced so much trial and error that there was no time for sleep.

Angel spent most of his mere week-long stay in the factory city developing the Equipment, and his prototype was not finished until after they'd moved out of the lodging facilities.

"And so through trial and error, I finally came up with this piece of equipment."

Everyone's baffled gaze was set on Angel, who wore the prototype. On his back was an ill-formed canister made from linked empty cans, and on his hip was the main unit, attached to him like a waist bag.

I feel kind of embarrassed looking like this...

Even Angel was willing to admit it, but that was not all he had on, as under his left armpit hung a holster. In it, though, was not a gun, but a controller that operated the Equipment. While it was similar to a gun in appearance, it did not shoot bullets. Instead, it fired a sharp anchor made from Iron Bamboo that had a wire attached to it.

"That's some heavy-duty gear."

Xenophon stared at Angel closely as if he were looking at a rare animal. Angel felt mildly abashed, but he knew that appearance did not always dictate performance.

"So, how do you use that machine? And more importantly, what's it for?!" Solm demanded with a dubious expression.

"Using it is simple."

Angel removed the controller from its holster and pointed the muzzle toward the second floor of the lodging facility.

"You aim at your target like you would aim a gun, then pull the lever on the controller."

As he pulled, the Equipment on his hips began to moan, and the anchor shot out from the muzzle. It bit into the wall like the claws of a predatory bird.

"Then, all you do is move the lever back, and..."

As Angel explained, he eased his grip on the controller's lever. Yet, perhaps because he was still unaccustomed and didn't properly calibrate the maneuver, the Equipment responded by spewing out all of its compressed gas. With the roar of a raging animal, it quickly began reeling the wire back in.

Oh no.

It was already too late by the time he realized what was happening.

Freed from the shackles of gravity, Angel's body flew into the air.

"Wuh?!"

His body swept up so suddenly, his consciousness wavered from the pressure. He started to feel faint and his vision grew dark, but he opened his eyes wide and avoided passing out through sheer force of will.

He quickly adjusted the controller to reduce the wire's retrieval rate, but his momentum was not as easy to manage. Angel crashed into the wall.

"Well, that's how this machine lets you move vertically." His entire body cried out in pain, but he acted as if nothing was wrong and continued his explanation. "This will let us fight eye-to-eye with them. I bet even the Titans will be stunned."

Angel extended the wire to return to the ground, then pulled in the anchor and returned it to the controller.

It was a wild demonstration, but the Equipment was functioning without any problems. If there was anything that needed work, it was its user.

"How many meters will that thing let you move?" Solm bit, in an apparent show of interest.

"Thirty meters."

"So you can't scale the Wall in one go."

"I'll be working on that in the future. The longer the wire, the heavier the Equipment gets, so I won't feel comfortable until we have lighter and sturdier materials."

"You come up with some interesting ideas." Solm nodded repeatedly.

"Don't forget about my short sword. If you combine it with his invention, you should be able to fight on a whole new level."

Xenophon took the short sword he had spent countless hours sharpening out of its scabbard and held it aloft. The silvery-white blade glinted in the sunlight.

"Doesn't it seem to be begging you to wield it?"

"Put that thing away before you start cuddling against it. You might shave your face off."

The edge of the Iron Bamboo sword appeared flawless and combat-ready. Xenophon's smug expression may have been irritating, but he had earned his bragging rights.

"Don't forget the stove!" Corina turned her back to everyone and pointed to the backpack she wore. The stove must have been shoved inside the distended bag.

"Looks like it's going to burst."

"I brought a bunch of fuel."

Xenophon clutched himself as he began to shake. "Just no explosions, please. Death by exploding Iceburst Stone might seem funny until it actually happens."

"Well, I guess it's the most practical item of the three. I don't know if they'll sell Iceburst Stone to civilians, though."

The craftsmen looked over each other's results, then boarded the wagon with satisfied expressions on their faces.

***

The group seemed inured to the travel sickness they'd suffered on their earlier trip, as they were able to converse and enjoy the scenery during the ride home. They could thank the skirmish with the anti-establishment forces for that, though it was a drastic way to treat nausea.

Still, they felt a tinge of anxiety. Despite the attack by the anti-establishment forces, the number of guards accompanying them had not changed. Considering the earlier battle, they could not help but feel that four cavalry was less than they needed; the lineup didn't seem intended to defend the craftsmen at all costs. Of course, the soldiers, headed by Solm, would fight to the end for Angel and the others, and two had in fact lost their lives in the earlier battle, but evidently what was important for the politicians was the factory city, not craftsmen. Rather than guards, it may have been more accurate to call the soldiers "escorts." Caspar wasn't far from the mark when he called them "navigators." At least the contingent had been replenished.

While there was cause for anxiety, there were no signs of an assault by anti-establishment forces, and the company arrived in Trost District, their halfway point, at midday. Unlike their earlier trip, they were on time. They ate and rested there, then left for Shiganshina District.

***

By the time the gate leading into Shiganshina District came into sight, the sun was setting far to the west. Though the crimson sky resembled coke burning in a furnace, it was getting colder by the moment. Their breaths were snow-white, and sitting still made them shrink into themselves. At most, there seemed to be another hour of daylight left.

"We've been gone a whole week. It doesn't feel like it at all," Corina said.

The others in the carriage agreed.

"We might have been in the factory city, but it was no different from being in the workshop as far as working went. The sad habits of a craftsman," Xenophon lamented.

"Also known as being a development geek."

Corina's shoulders sagged. "I was hoping for a vacation when we left…"

"If only there had been some amusement facility," concurred Xenophon. "But it was still under construction."

"I bet we'd have busted our asses anyway. The old man wouldn't just decide to give us a vacation, you know?"

"I suppose you're right…" Corina mourned, visibly convinced.

By the time their chat ended, they had approached the gate.

If the gate that led outside the Wall was the front gate, then the one leading to the interior could be called the back gate. The portals were positioned perfectly opposite each other, and if they continued in a straight line, they would reach the front or main gate. The difference was that only one of the gates stood open. With no particular reason to defend it, there were fewer guards here as well.

"I'm going to use the portable stove for dinner tonight. I'm sure it'll make my parents happy."

"The big shots, too. They'll be happy enough to cry."

Only a tiny fraction of citizens knew about the Iceburst Stone, a brand new material with no set use. Its enriching the dinner tables of regular households was a long shot.

"Wouldn't you say it's a bit restive, though?" Xenophon tilted his head as soon as they passed through the back gate. "I somehow find it hard to believe that we'd have a welcoming party waiting for our return..."

As they peeked out from the driver's seat, there was a din in the air as if everyone was gossiping. The avenue was, as always, full of people, but this wasn't the usual hustle and bustle. A mood like viscous muck seemed to be pooling.

"Looks like something happened," Solm said grimly as he pointed forward. They could see Wall Maria and the main gate ahead of them, but he was trying to call attention to something else, a huge mass of people there from whom the commotion seemed to stem.

I have a bad feeling about this...

Angel felt his chest knot. He couldn't tell exactly what was going on because of the distance, but it seemed to be some sort of gathering.

"Could it be a Survey Corps parade?"

As Corina observed, it closely resembled a Survey Corps expedition's return. Yet, the throng was larger, over a thousand people in size.

"The Survey Corps lost a large number of men during their last expedition. It would take longer for them to reorganize," reminded Xenophon.

"So they'd be in no shape to go on an expedition, huh? What's that, then?"

In addition to the citizens assembled in front of the main gate, they could also make out soldiers. Perhaps there had been some trouble and the two sides seemed to be arguing, in some places scuffling. The clash appeared to be widening.

A citizens' protest? It wasn't rare to see citizens voicing their dissatisfaction with the regime through demonstrations. *This is too big for a protest, though...*

There was danger in the air as if a riot could break out at any moment.

"Let's check it out."

Solm slowly drove the carriage forward.

As they approached the mass of people, they started to get a better idea of the situation. The individuals there were indeed residents, but they seemed agitated, their eyes bloodshot, their breathing ragged. They wore black priest-like robes and let out bizarre shouts toward Wall Maria that sounded like chants. Their movements, nearly as regulated as the soldiers' perhaps thanks to a crowd mentality, also exuded an erratic vibe as though they were dreaming.

"Something is strange about those people..." Corina frowned in clear discomfort.

"Yeah, creepy."

Xenophon was observing the grotesque crowd as carefully as if he were appraising a product. "Looks like there has been a hell of a complication while we were gone."

"Who are those people?"

"I think it's clear enough from their actions."

"All they're doing is facing the Wall and shouting." Hearing his own words, it suddenly came to Angel. "Wall Lovers..." It was one of the terms used to ridicule those who deified the Walls.

"Not them. I think they have the same roots, though."

"Stop acting so stuck up and just tell me."

The carriage had approached the front gate while they were talking. Given the mass of people they had to stop a hundred meters away, but they were still close enough to see what was going on.

In front of the gate stood a woman whom Angel had seen before, her back to the wall. "Elena Mansell..."

She wore black clothes that resembled mourning garb. She stood completely still with hollow eyes.

"Someone you know?"

"Kind of," Angel answered vaguely as he focused on Elena. It seemed as though she still couldn't accept Heath's death, and there was no sense of vitality to her. Her expression was flat and mask-like.

What's she up to?

Angel tried to figure out the situation based on Elena's demeanor, but before he managed to, she made a move. Her voice defied one's imagination, so loud was it for someone with her frame.

"I—we have but one wish. Open these gates immediately, that is all we ask!"

"Hunh?" Angel grunted involuntarily at her ridiculous request. He could have thought for days and not have arrived at such a conclusion. "Has she gone crazy?"

"I doubt that she or the people with her would say so."

"Who are those people?!" interjected Corina.

"Oh? You still haven't figured it out? Well, those people are—"

"Titan Lovers."

Solm clicked his tongue.

"I see. So they're the ones who worship the Titans." Angel had heard rumors of them but had simply dismissed it as a tall tale. No sane person would ever deify and worship the Titans.

It was only a few decades ago that humanity had been driven to near extinction. No matter how much they loved the Titans, the Titans surely only saw them as food. Opening the gate was nothing short of risible.

"Open the gates! And let us be united with the great Titans!!"

The believers greeted Elena's voice with shouts.

"Why is this happening?" Solm's expression was growing more sour by the moment. There was no humor to be found in a former team leader's bride falling for the Titans.

"They're quick to exploit openings in people's hearts to bring them into the fold. It was probably useful for them to have someone related to the Survey Corps join them."

"And so this rally."

Elena joining them may have encouraged them to mount a showdown instead of continuing on with their modest underground activities. It was clear that the believers were serious about their demands as they had placed a number of facilities under their influence.

This is going to be a pain…

No amount of logic would sway people with completely different values. To them, it was Angel that was simply a heretic.

"Why are the soldiers not doing anything?" implored Corina.

"They probably want to but can't," explained Xenophon.

There were enough troops mustered in front of the main gate to deal with an uprising. Soldiers from the Garrison, the protectors of the Walls, were there, of course, as well as men and women from the Survey Corps and the Military Police Brigade. The troop presence was so robust that it would be easy to quell any riot. They just stood and watched, however, and showed no signs of moving to subdue the believers.

"It seems as though they have a hostage."

Xenophon pointed to a watchtower built on top of the Wall. It was occupied by a number of believers who held a blade to the throat of a portly middle-aged man. His plump body and well-tailored clothes suggested that he was one of the wealthy.

"Who is that?"

"He's an official from the royal government," Solm spat out, annoyed.

Ah, one of the shut-ins then.

Solm wouldn't be irritated by just any affiliation with the royal government.

"Probably here to be wined and dined," Xenophon noted. "Look at that slovenly body of his. He seems to be living quite the life of refinement."

"He's certainly not eating canned food."

"Well, you have to wonder how he was being entertained."

"Some beautiful woman must have catered to him for his meals."

Angel glanced at Elena.

"I see. That does seem likely."

While Angel and Xenophon saw fit to banter, the tussling between the believers and the soldiers by the main gate seemed to be moments away from getting out of control. If they couldn't be neutralized quickly, they all faced the worst-case scenario, the gates opening.

So the problem here is the hostage.

The soldiers were unable to make their move thanks to the official who had fallen into the believers' hands.

Not that I care about what happens to him…

The death of an incompetent only interested in political bargaining, who knew nothing about how things were on the ground, did no real harm. The soldiers were under the control of the royal government, however, and could not afford to see it that way.

"I know we just returned, but you should escape to somewhere safe. This place is about to turn into a battlefield."

Right as Solm urged the others, out of the blue Liberty Bell loudly rang out.

"Give us true freedom!" Elena shouted at the top of her lungs.

"Give us true freedom!" The believers followed in chorus. Their voices soon grew so loud that they drowned out the sound of the bell.

What in the world is going on…

Then, as they were standing by idly, it happened.

The believers decapitated the official.

Wall Maria was stained red by the blood that gushed forth. Perhaps it had some sort of ritual meaning. As soon as this blood offering was made, something incredible happened.

"The gates…are opening…"

Whether or not the believers' ardent wishes had reached heaven, the gates started to crack open.

It was operating smoothly. Careful maintenance had backfired, and the town was laid bare and defenseless within moments.

"Give us true freedom!" the believers cheered, rushing into the opening.

"No!"

Solm drew his short sword from its scabbard on his hip and began charging toward the main gate.

Now that the hostage was killed and the gates were open, the time to keep watching and waiting was over. Solm pushed straight through the crowds toward the gate, and various units followed him. While they were headed to the watchtower on top of the Wall where the equipment that opened and closed the gate was, the area by the front gate was a mess of soldiers and believers, making it difficult to even approach Wall Maria, let alone the watchtower. The soldiers had an overwhelming advantage when it came to individual skill, but the believers held a superior position. Fighting off the believers, getting to the top of the Wall, then going on to retake the watchtower meant the troops needed a significant amount of time to establish control.

"Let's find somewhere safe."

Not because they were in danger of getting involved in the battle. As long as the gates were open, being in the district was no safer than being outside the Walls.

"Indeed. We should turn tail and run."

"Run…to where?"

"Anywhere farther in."

At the moment, any location would do. Angel tried to set the carriage in motion, but the avenue was jammed full of soldiers, believers, and people scrambling for safety. It was no place to be using a carriage to get around.

"I guess we'll have to walk…"

Angel hurriedly shouldered the gas cylinder, wrapped the Equipment around his waist, and attached the controller. Next to his life, there was nothing more important to him than the Equipment he had developed, and there was no way he was leaving it behind. Xenophon must have felt similarly, holding on to his short sword as if his life depended on it. Corina was the only one who decided to abandon her luggage.

By the time they got off the carriage, the town was already starting to show signs of impending chaos. The soldiers and believers had already been squaring off, and the air had been uneasy from the moment they arrived, but the opening of the gates immediately brought the sense of tension that surrounded them to new heights. It was natural for the citizens to act as they did. That the gates should be opened due to a riot was simply beyond their imagination.

If we don't hurry, they're going to all start panicking.

That would give rise to unforeseen events and accidents. But the biggest fear of all was that they would soon be faced with uninvited guests.

They'll be here if we don't do something.

Ignoring Angel's unease, the believers wore gleeful expressions as they rushed beyond the Wall. For the men and women that worshipped the Titans, the outside world was a holy land, even a paradise. To Angel's eyes, though, their actions seemed like tossing feed into a fish tank. It was clear that the hungry Titans would be drawn to the bait and approach the town.

We have to run. We have to…

But the road was congested, and they could only move forward slowly.

Everyone's thinking the same thing.

Still, they had no other choice but to simply move forward.

As Angel headed toward the back gate, he suddenly heard a wave of cheers, screams, and shrieks coming from behind him.

The moment his body turned to meet the voices, Angel shivered. The blow was so brutal that he felt as though his heart was being torn in two. He gushed forth a soundless shriek.

"Aahh…"

Angel gulped, and his eyes jolted wide open. The understanding of the world he'd built up over his eighteen years of life came crumbling apart with a roar.

For a moment, he couldn't understand what had happened. Or rather, he didn't want to understand. His thought processes had shut down, and his mind grew as blank as a white canvas.

Once he somehow managed to put his thoughts back together, he took notice of a man who was pushing through the front gate.

"What *is* that…" Angel pushed the words out from his throat.

A middle-aged man one might see on the street had emerged at the front gate. While his calm face and figure offered no cause for surprise, he was nonetheless utterly different.

"A monster…"

The man was so large that it was not a stretch to use the word. No human being even came close. His size, reaching for the clouds, sufficed to impart an illusion that a mountain was writhing forth. His body was

as tall as the gates, roughly ten meters in height. Faced with this over-whelming being that seemed to defy the laws of nature, Angel could do nothing but stand dead still.

It was either a god or a demon.

Now he could understand why the believers would want to worship them.

"So that's a Titan…"

The Titan lazily stumbled through the gates.

Perhaps having no concept of civilization, the Titan was completely nude, and his protruding stomach rippled every time he walked. It went without saying what his stomach was filled of. He trampled multiple people to death with every step he took. No doubt excited by all the prey that he saw, a look of utter bliss had spread across the Titan's face.

He stomped on the believers that offered their prayers to him as if they were worms and smashed with his palms any soldiers trying to put up a fight. There was no hesitation in his actions. Perhaps the Titan was driven to eat humans by instinct, as he greedily gobbled up one after the next. He either had no sense of taste, or the clothes and weapons he uncaringly ate together with the humans acted as spices.

Mammon.

The term suddenly bubbled up in the back of Angel's mind. The hoggish, gorging, gluttonous, and greedy Titan, the incarnation of a nightmare, wore the glowing smile of an innocent infant. The sight ter-rified Angel.

Now that the Titan had been allowed to enter the town, it had be-come a crucible of chaos. The residents of Shiganshina District had, in theory, lived there aware of the risks, but they must have never thought that a Titan would actually be allowed in. The idea of one strolling straight through the main gate was utterly absurd. Terrified by their im-pending doom, the people of Shiganshina pushed toward their one route of escape, the back gate. There was no room for the spirit of sharing.

"Trying to escape right now doesn't seem like a very good idea," Xenophon conceded.

With thousands of residents surging toward the back gate, escaping

85

seemed like a tall order. The gate was acting as a bottleneck, creating a huge backup. The people had been terrified into a state of delirium and were desperate to get even a single step closer to the gate. Morals and ethics had turned to dust in the wind as their survival instincts simply pushed others aside. Approaching the scene promised much more than some cuts and bruises.

As the people of Shiganshina worked in agony to escape, Mammon kept up his massacre. The Titan sauntered north through the town as he slew and devoured. There was nothing that could stand in his way. He destroyed buildings with complete ease, as if they were made from toy blocks, leaving mountains of rubble and bodies in his trail. He was like a walking disaster. While it was hard to imagine that humans could do anything to fight against the Titan, soldiers still challenged him with their useless blades. They were literally unable even to scratch him. Never mind slicing through his skin, their weapons simply bounced off of the Titan. His body was so tough it was as if he were covered in chain mail.

"No effect…" Corina shrunk to the ground in shock.

"So we've been up against…true monsters."

"It's no surprise that the Survey Corps suffers such huge losses," concurred Xenophon.

They now truly understood why it was necessary to have a gigantic wall like Wall Maria. Without one, every last human would have been eaten by the Titans ages ago.

Having killed many, perhaps bored with his now-sparse surroundings, the Titan began to move to a new location with more humans to feed on. He ran with the quickness of a wild beast chasing after prey, the movements at odds with the dull and slow image his appearance implied. It was nowhere near a human's sprint. He looked able to outrun even a horse.

His face still stretched into a beaming smile as though he'd just run into his best friend, the Titan continued to charge down the avenue, rushing forth like a surging wave, destroying everything in his path. Before Angel and the others had an opportunity to flee, the Titan had drawn close.

The Titan was big. That much was already obvious, but he was so gargantuan in size that it made Angel take notice of the fact all over again. He was so huge that his feet alone filled Angel's field of vision.

It was too bizarre a scene. As though overwhelmed by the Titan's noxious presence, Angel's body locked up and his knees began to chatter. While his instincts had constantly been telling him to run, his body was still as if pinned down. The same had happened to Xenophon and Corina. They stood absolutely still like their bodies had been hardened with plaster. Their faces were a sickly pale color, and the vitality had seemingly been sucked from them by their sense of despair. What they saw before them was simply too absurd and threatened to make them regret they'd been born into this world at all. Keeping calm under the circumstances was an impossible feat.

The Titan raised a muscular arm overhead.

Run...

Angel tried to jolt himself into action, but his body was too busy shaking to move a single inch.

The Titan swung down his arm.

Move... Move...

Angel somehow broke his arms free of the chains of fear that had bound his mind, slamming both of them into his knees. The dull pain spread through both knees, and the feeling cured his trembling.

"Move!"

Angel braced his legs as he shouted, then kicked off from the ground to jump perfectly sideways. Moments later, the Titan's fist smashed into the ground. A sound echoed like a cannonball striking home, and the ground rumbled. The pulverized road scattered in all directions together with clouds of dust. If he had been any slower, Angel would have surely been crushed.

Still, Angel was not yet out of harm's way. The Titan slowly pulled back the balled hand he had buried into the ground. Fragments of the smashed road seemed to have cut through his skin, as fresh blood trickled down from his fist.

"Are you okay?" Angel yelled to his companions after regaining his bearings.

"Somehow…" While he was choking on the dust that filled the air, Xenophon seemed unscathed.

"Are you all right, Corina?"

There was no reply.

"Corina?"

Angel looked around. Corina, who just moments ago was next to him, had suddenly disappeared as if spirited away. A chill ran up his spine.

DRIP, DRIP.

Blood trickled down the Titan's fist.

Terrified, Angel looked down toward the ground.

Where the Titan's fist had caused it to cave in lay a lump of crushed meat.

"Corina…"

The hunk of meat so little resembled its former shape that he was only able to tell it was her from the work clothes that covered it. Bones all over her body had been broken, and what her cracked skull had once contained protruded out. It was instantly obvious that she was dead. The Titan grabbed the lump that used to be Corina with his fingers then brought it to his mouth. He wriggled his mouth and tossed Corina's head aside like he was plucking a stem from a fruit. There was no trace of respect for the dead in his casual gesture. Spotting food on the ground, he'd picked up and eaten it, that was all.

"Damn it!" Angel spat, bit his lip, and glared at the Titan. Blood rushed to his head, and his body burned as though it had been thrown onto a fire.

The Titans were dreadful. Being near one was enough to freeze your body and threaten your sanity. But at that moment, Angel's feelings of dread were overwhelmed by his hatred for the Titan. His desire to do harm anesthetized his fear.

"Give me the blade!" Angel barked.

Xenophon stood stock still, his eyes wide open.

"Xenophon!" Angel yelled again.

The man's mouth just shook open and closed like a fish trying to breathe, his empty eyes fixed on the dripping blood.

"Xenophon, give me the blade!!" Angel screamed as if rebuking him. This finally brought him to his senses.

Xenophon immediately tossed the short sword he gripped to Angel, who caught it, removed it from its sheath, and approached the Titan's feet. He didn't know how to fight, but even if he did, any standard tactics were surely worthless against the monster that stood before him. In that case, there was only one thing to do.

Angel slashed at the Titan's ankles with all of his might. The blade sliced through the Titan's skin with little resistance, opening a wound that laid bare bright red meat and the bones it surrounded.

"You did it!" Xenophon exulted, but that was the extent of the damage. In fact, it was hard to tell if Angel had even truly hurt his foe. The Titan showed no signs of being in pain, and moreover, the wound let out a white, steam-like smoke and began to scab over before their very eyes. It would have taken a human two to three months to recover from the deep cut, yet it healed as Angel watched.

"Damned monster…"

But Titans were organisms just like humans. Despite unusual recuperative powers, they wouldn't survive a blow to a vital spot. The only problem was that Angel didn't know where that might be.

Crap… Is it just pointless?

Short of a suicide attack, there was nothing left that Angel could do. He did, however, notice something after seeing a Titan for himself. The creatures were even less intelligent than he had imagined. They showed no interest whatsoever in how humans lived, only reacting to any food they saw in front of them. They captured and ate humans. That was all. Even dogs and cats seemed far smarter than the Titans.

While hardly a breakthrough discovery to turn the tables then and there, identifying a point where humans were superior was big. Being more intelligent, in particular, was an advantage that offered prospects of winning. Moreover, it was a defining human characteristic. With full use of their intelligence, they might be able to control, if not outright defeat, the Titans.

As Angel reached this conclusion, he had a flash of inspiration.

"Hey, freak! Just try and eat me!" Angel jeered at the Titan, waving at him as if to taunt him, and began running toward the main gate. The Titan seemed to accept Angel's challenge and began to chase after him.

Angel's plan was simple.

If I can't defeat it, I just need to get it out of town.

The Titans hewed to a clear behavioral principle: eating humans, nothing more or less.

Show 'em bait and they'll give chase out of instinct.

Of course, Angel would be acting as the bait.

The carriage they had abandoned earlier came into view. The horse appeared excited but not out of control. It looked like he could drive immediately.

Angel stepped into the driver's seat and immediately whipped the horse into action.

Just as he had hoped, the Titan came after him. Angel's original plan was to head straight forward to exit through the main gate, but the road was piled too high with corpses for the carriage to pass through. Angel moved from the driver's seat to the horse's back, then used the short sword to cut loose the harness connecting the horse to the carriage. Freed, the horse became more maneuverable, and Angel headed for the main gate skillfully avoiding obstacles.

"Angel!"

He looked toward the voice. Maria and the other Garrison soldiers had just taken the watchtower back from the believers. Seeing this, he pushed his horse to move even faster.

As they had not discussed his plan, Maria didn't necessarily understand Angel's intentions. But considering the Garrison's duties, there was only one thing for her to do.

Angel passed through the main gate.

Before him stretched a barren, untouched plain. It was uncertain where all the believers who exited the walls had gone, but a number were now corpses, crushed by the Titan. Other than those bodies, though, he could see nothing worth taking note of. Perhaps there were unknown countries and peoples beyond the horizon, or even the holy land that the believers sought, but nothing Angel saw hinted at their existence.

It was a once-in-a-lifetime chance to see the world outside of the Walls, but this was no time to satisfy his curiosity. Angel stopped his horse and used the reins to make it face the gate. Some compared the human world to a birdcage, and he could see why, looking at it from outside the Wall. In fact, a birdcage would be a step up since caged birds could at least see the outside world.

It's like a prison.

Albeit the significant difference in scope, men and women were forced to live in there surrounded on all sides by walls—the very definition of a prison.

Soon, the avatar of fear appeared from the main gate.

"There you are, monster…"

As soon as he faced the Titan, the gates began to roar shut.

Looks like you got the idea, Maria.

Considering the Garrison's mission, she had no choice but to close the gates. Placing Angel and Shiganshina District on a scale, it was obvious which way the balance tipped. Yet, Angel hadn't dashed past the Wall in order to become a noble sacrifice.

"You know, common sense isn't etched in stone. That's what technology's for."

Angel pulled the Equipment controller from its holster and pointed it toward Wall Maria. He didn't need to aim carefully. His target was so immense that he could have hit it with his eyes closed. As he pressed the lever on the controller, the Equipment began to hum, shooting an anchor with the speed of an arrow deep into the wall, about twenty meters above the ground.

"I'll rewrite the common sense that you can't defeat the Titans!"

With the controller's lever returned to its original position, the Equipment began to wind in the wire at an incredible rate. Angel's body was flung into the air, freed from gravity's yoke.

But there was a price to pay for actually moving in such an impossible manner. Angel's body was met with enough pressure to nearly incapacitate him. Perhaps due to not enough blood flowing to his head, his vision tunneled and the world began to turn gray. Angel grit his teeth and pushed through the pressure, adjusting his posture and fine-tuning his speed with the lever.

Until yesterday, entering and exiting through the gates was common sense. Starting today, though, things are going to be different.

Angel flashed past the Titan's flank, and Wall Maria approached ahead of him. He balanced himself and made a soft landing against the Wall, then yanked himself upward. His body quickly rose toward high ground, where the Titan could not reach him. But shortly before his destination, the gas cylinder on his back made an odd noise like air was being let out of it.

"Gas leak…"

Something was wrong with the cylinder, whether it was shoddy welding or a structural defect. In any case, the gas leak caused the Equipment to stop operating. Angel moved the lever but there was no reaction, and he was left dangling eighteen meters above the ground.

"Damn it! Not now!!"

Malfunctions were part and parcel of prototypes, but Angel could not help but curse. He looked down to see the Titan reaching out to grab him. Jumping up may have allowed the Titan to do so, but the creature did not seem intelligent enough for that. While Angel had narrowly escaped death, he was still not free from danger. He had to somehow get over the Wall.

"Oh boy…"

If he had his tools, he could disassemble the Equipment and improvise something, but he had nothing at hand. All of his tools were in the carriage. He was hardly in a spot to tinker, either, dangling in the air like a bagworm.

Suddenly, his body sunk ten centimeters or so. He looked above his head to see that the wire supporting his body had started to fray. He had used multiple thin strands weaved together as one in order to ensure its strength, but even that, it appeared, hadn't been enough. The wire frayed one strand at a time making an awful noise. It was only a matter of time before it could no longer hold his weight.

"Oh no…"

Right as Angel seemed doomed, a rope came dangling down from above.

"Grab on!"

His eyes followed the rope up to the top of the Wall, where he could see Maria's face peeking out. Her expression was difficult to describe, a jumble of emotions from appalled to irate. Angel was sure he was in for an extended chewing-out later, but it surely beat ending up dead.

As soon as he wrapped the rope around his arm, he started being pulled up. In the meantime, Angel met eyes with the Titan, who was still smiling from cheek to cheek.

"What're you so happy about?"

The Titan kept smiling even though Angel, his meal, was getting away.

"Are you still going to be smiling like that when I kill you?" Angel challenged, but the Titan merely smiled, not deigning a reply.

The sun was sinking below the horizon.

A horde of humanity's sworn enemies was advancing toward them, drawn, no doubt, by the believers who had rushed outside the Wall. It was a desperate vista hinting to any who saw it that the end was nigh.

CHAPTER THREE

A Titan invasion was an unprecedented incident that plunged the people of Shiganshina District into the depths of fear.

The morning after, the town looked like a literal hell on Earth. The killed, wounded, and missing numbered as high as five thousand in total. Piles of corpses waiting to be collected sat casually on roads stained a dark red with their blood. The low temperature kept the bodies from rotting quickly so there was no fear of an epidemic as long as they could be dealt with in a timely manner, but the sight was more than enough to corrode the survivors' hearts.

While the Titan had been overpowering, its victims were only twenty percent of the whole. The rest fell in a man-made disaster caused by panic, namely a stampede resulting from the narrow escape path. The majority of the victims were those unable to defend themselves, such as children and elderly people, who were crushed to death.

Serious damage had also been done to buildings, with as many as a hundred homes completely or partially destroyed. Flames could still be seen in places around the city, and it was estimated that the final toll would be twice the current number. Plans to rebuild them were not yet on the horizon.

While massive damage had been dealt to homes, Wall Maria was left completely unscratched. The main gate was in good shape as well. It was ironic, then, that the myth of safety had nevertheless been demolished. It was an unforeseen situation for the corps and the royal government, and any trust the people had in them took a nosedive. While the cultists responsible for the turmoil had been subdued by the soldiers, that did not mean the incident had been resolved. In fact, it was only the beginning, with investigations to come.

Elena, who had incited the believers, was found dead near the front gate. She had been eaten, then vomited out by the Titan. While her corpse was covered in bodily fluids, it was nearly unscathed. It was possible that the Titan had gulped her down whole. Titans ate but did not digest humans, filling their stomachs with men and women, vomiting them back out, then repeating the cycle again. Traces of this behavior had been left around the town. Like a cat bringing up hairballs after grooming, the Titan had hacked up lumps of human bodies.

The incident had laid many problems bare, causing the people of Shiganshina to erupt into discontent, but by promising extensive recovery work and even greater assistance than before, the royal government managed to evade calls for accountability. The residents had no choice but to prioritize their own lives, and so the issues raised went unresolved and forgotten.

***

The setting sun blazed red as it lit the graveyard. The space, over five hundred square meters in size, served as the resting place for those who had passed away in the incident.

It was doubtful, though, that they were resting in peace. The mass grave was hastily built as a way to handle the corpses that inundated the city. No time had been expended on thoughts of showing respect for the deceased. Public health concerns took precedence, but even then, it was a rough measure. There was a memorial stone but no inscription, leaving it unclear as to who was buried there.

"I'm not really a flowers guy, but…" Angel placed some on the altar and breathed a heavy sigh.

Corina, who, along with a number of his other colleagues, had died in the turmoil, rested in the graveyard. While they could only bury Corina's head, others were missing with no remains to be found whatsoever, and some had suffered so much damage that they could not be identified. Compared to them, things could have turned out worse for her.

But it really only matters to the survivors…

The only ones who could be saved by praying in front of the graves were those still alive. The dead felt nothing.

"Were you able to contact Corina's family?"

Angel stared at the memorial for a moment, then shifted his eyes sideways. There stood Solm and Maria, who had known her, as well as Xenophon.

"I tried visiting her home, but it had been destroyed."

Maria seemed exhausted, perhaps from the reconstruction work that was still taking place every day. Removing rubble was bone-breaking labor in itself, but she must have been discovering remains during the process. It had to be difficult work, both physically and emotionally. That she had been unable to protect the town must be weighing heavily on her as well.

"I did some looking, too, but I couldn't figure out where her parents were. I just hope they've evacuated somewhere."

"It's possible they've already been reunited," Xenophon said while looking at the memorial. It was an inappropriate remark, but considering the circumstances, it was a possibility.

"She was too young to die. She had so much ahead of her as a craftsman…"

Corina herself could not have imagined being eaten and killed by a Titan.

"Apparently, the conservatives have gained a lot of influence in the wake of this incident. I can see this being a pain," Solm scowled.

"What, are they talking about dissolving the Survey Corps like always?"

"They want to seal the gates," Maria sighed, then continued, "The incident occurred because there's a gate, so if we just sealed the gates…"

"Then no one would try anything crazy? That's pretty simplistic, even for them," Xenophon said with a stunned expression.

"Even if they did that, there'll still be idiots trying to go outside. It just means more work for us if there aren't any gates."

"Yes. They want to leave through the gate because it's there. If it isn't, their target will shift to all of Wall Maria."

"Just like the Titans," Angel pointed out. "Without Shiganshina

District, their bait, we won't be able to predict their movements. Our soldiers can't patrol the entire Wall, can they?"

"Think you could tell that to the bigwigs?"

"If they'll listen to what a petty little citizen has to say." In other words, it was hopeless. "Ultimately, our only option is to do something about the Titans. Humanity's situation is just going to get worse at this rate."

"Do something about them? We can't defeat them…" reminded Maria.

"That's not true. There's hope." Xenophon showed everyone his short sword.

"Is that the sword you were talking about?"

"Oh, that's right. You don't know how sharp it is, do you, Solm?"

"What do you mean?"

"When he and I were attacked by the Titan…this thing came in mighty handy," declared Xenophon. While that was open to debate, the blade had certainly sliced though the Titan's flesh.

"I see. So it's an effective weapon against a Titan."

"You can't kill a Titan just by cutting it," Maria objected.

"They do recover so fast it's unfair. I can understand why it became common sense that they're immortal," Angel agreed, but he still wasn't convinced. "Yesterday's common sense is today's nonsense. I'll flip the 'fact' that they're immortal upside down."

"Indeed. That's why our craft exists."

While Solm and Maria looked conflicted, Angel and Xenophon were feeling motivated.

"But before we can take the Titans on, we need to know them better. The Titans are clearly organisms, so they must have a weakness."

"So we find it and stab it with this." Xenophon made a thrusting motion with the short sword.

"There's too much we don't know about the Titans."

"Yes. All we really know is that they eat humans."

"That's why we need to conduct a thorough investigation of their behavior. I'm sure we'll find a clue."

But it wouldn't be like observing an animal.

We need to secure the corps' help somehow.

In particular, of the Survey Corps. Studying the Titans' behavior required working outside the Wall.

"Couldn't you undertake a behavioral study of the Titans during an expedition?"

"The conclusion of our investigations is that the Titans are unkill-able. It'll be hard to overturn it."

"But we have to."

If no possibility whatsoever existed, humanity had no future, and Corina would not be able to rest in peace.

"Introduce us to your boss."

"The commander?"

"You said to tell the bigwigs, right? We may not have the connections to talk to the royal government, but we might have a chance with the Survey Corps. After all, we have a corpsman right here."

Solm sunk into thought for a moment after hearing his friend's proposal.

"Don't get your hopes up," he replied.

***

Angel was diligently working in his development lab to fix the Equipment. While it had yielded even better results than expected, sparing Angel's life as a result, it was still not ready for field use. The gas cylinder had leaked, and there were problems with the wire's strength. Repairs would not be enough to ready it for the battlefield. Large-scale improvements were needed.

"I didn't expect it to be so hard to simply meet with the commander, though," Xenophon complained, scanning the lab.

"I thought he'd at least see us… I guess I was naïve." If their proposal had been shot down, it would have been one thing, but not even being granted an audience meant the end of the story. "That's the problem with chain of command."

"And Solm's toward the bottom of it. He'd be seen as arrogant if he tried to talk to the commander." The standard practice would be to go through a team leader, who would go to the deputy commander, who would then talk to the commander. Those in titled positions held discretionary power, and Solm's request hadn't even made it past the team leader.

"I think we have a timing problem, too."

"Yes, they have their hands full rebuilding the town."

While all the bodies had been buried and the rubble cleared out, the damaged buildings were just starting to be rebuilt. It would be months until the city was returned to how it once looked. Considering that priority, it seemed obvious that their request would be denied.

"I doubt they will be going on any expeditions for the time being, either. Right now, it would just open them up to criticism."

"So we'll just have to wait for our opportunity, huh?"

"If you devote yourself to development, it'll come before you know it."

"Yeah…" Angel agreed with Xenophon, but he couldn't give up so easily. There was no guarantee that they'd begin studying the Titans once the town was rebuilt.

I need to somehow press them to go on an expedition…

But he couldn't think of a single method.

A way to move the Survey Corps into action. Hmm… That would be bold, even for me.

Though shocked by his own idea, he began giving serious thought to his method.

***

"Great, but this is the last time. Okay?" Maria let out a deep sigh as she glared at Angel.

"Looks better on me than you'd think, huh?" he puffed his chest out as if to show off the clothes he wore. They weren't his regular work clothes; he was wearing the military uniform of a Garrison soldier.

"Where did you get that?"

"You'd get mad if I told you."

"I'm already mad."

Maria was scowling, but she would surely become furious if she found out that he'd bought the clothes at a black market. While you could buy just about anything you wanted there, many of the items broke the law. A military uniform was simply out of the question.

"Good thing you're in the Garrison. Like they say, that's what friends are for."

"If they find you, we're not getting off with just a slap on the wrist."

"I'm used to it."

"I'm not!"

Maria was well within her rights to be indignant. She was to guide him to the watchtower, from where he'd observe the Titans—without permission, naturally.

I'd be in hot water if they found out.

In the worst case, he'd end up in a cell eating disgusting jail food.

Angel had considered different ways to get the Survey Corps to investigate the Titans but had come up empty. The solution he had devised instead was to investigate them himself. Of course, he was powerless on his own, which is why he'd gotten Maria involved.

"I'm not kidding when I say this is the only time."

As she emphasized the fact yet again, Wall Maria's main gate began to come into view. Wooden spiral staircases rose on both sides of the gates. Once they climbed up, the lookout tower came into view. Angel followed Maria with a nonchalant look as she entered the watchtower, relieving the soldier on night duty there. The soldier must have been tired from the night shift, as he paid no attention to Angel.

"I think that took a year off my life," Maria said as she put her hand to her chest and sighed in relief.

"That was easier than I thought."

"Maybe, but that doesn't mean we're doing this again."

"Yes, ma'am."

Angel shrugged, then looked toward the copper-red infertile plains.

It was a chilly sight, with nothing to catch the eye. Even if they could take the outside world back from the Titans, cultivating the starved soil, building a town, and thus creating a place suitable for humans to inhabit would take a considerable amount of time.

As he stared at the wasteland harder, Angel was able to make out a number of humanoid figures. He squinted his eyes and focused on the man-shaped monsters that lurked there.

Titans…

As soon as he could make them out, an intense feeling rushed through Angel's body, like his nerves had been doused in cold water. His entire body erupted in cold sweat, and he could feel his consciousness fading.

Can't…breathe…

In reality, it was just that he was forgetting to breathe. Angel nearly fainted but somehow managed to stay on his feet after taking a few panicked breaths.

Crap. So I'm scared of them?

He would have preferred never to see them again, but it was no time to be running scared.

I'll be the one…to defeat the Titans.

It was not some praiseworthy resolve for the sake of humanity. It was simply something he had to do. For Corina, who met a bitter death, and to wipe away the fear the Titans had implanted in him.

Angel roused himself and immediately began observing the Titans. The first thing he noticed was that Titans were not communal in nature. They moved alone in scattered locations and did not seem to congregate. He watched them for a while but saw no signs that they understood one another, nor did he see any regularity in their movements.

Some Titans walked around aimlessly, while others stood still and stared at the sky. They varied in size, and it seemed as though Mammon, the one who had broken into Shiganshina District, was large even among Titans. The smaller ones were about three meters tall, but that still made them significantly larger than a human.

"Are they always like that?"

"Yeah."

"I wonder what they eat to get that big."

"Who knows," Maria said, tilting her head to the side.

Angel had his doubts. "They must eat, right?"

"I think so."

"You've never seen them eat?"

"Apart from humans."

It seemed odd, as they would normally not have any chances to eat humans.

I guess if there was another country out there...

As long as Titans were organisms, they needed to take in some sort of nutrients. Not eating or drinking at all was untenable. Furthermore, there was their size. They would need a tremendous amount of energy in order to sustain themselves. There was no way that they did not eat.

"We're truly in the dark... It's no surprise that we can't defeat the Titans."

The more powerful the enemy, the more information you needed on them. Especially important was the enemy's weakness. Fighting without that knowledge would be truly foolhardy.

Maybe there was no need to defeat them.

Not studying the Titans' behavior must have been a choice made by the royal government. Or to be more exact, the conservatives. On the other hand, the Survey Corps held expeditions beyond the Walls. One could see in their actions glimpses of the reformist aim of retaking the land seized by the Titans.

In other words, a compromise.

Perhaps they had shelved the question of the Titans in order to avoid a confrontation so that the factions themselves may coexist. Of course, this also meant shelving the public interest. For the Survey Corps, who risked their lives with every expedition, it must have been an unbearable situation.

I don't care a whit about conservative or reformist.

Meanwhile, his best friend was in the Survey Corps. If the expeditions continued on unchanged, Solm could one day be killed by a Titan, and Maria would feel absolutely lost.

I'll be the one to expose the Titans' weakness.

So resolving, Angel stared at the outer lands.

***

Angel learned little about the Titans from up on the Wall. Looking at them through binoculars from afar only revealed their external characteristics. He hadn't gained a clue as to any weaknesses.

Still, there was one thing he noticed during his observations: expressions. Like humans, the Titans exhibited feelings. Unlike humans, though, each only showed one emotion. In other words, a Titan with a happy expression would always be wearing it, never indicating other states like anger or sadness. When he thought back on it, Mammon's expression had never changed, either. His smile had never left his face whether he was eating Corina or cut with a short sword. This realization didn't offer a way to defeat the Titans, though.

Maria only helped him once, but Angel wore his soldier's uniform and climbed to the top of the Wall many times. He meticulously observed the Titans each time, but his investigation was taking forever to progress. All he was finding was information that backed up things they already knew.

As Maria had said, the Titans never ate anything. Many animals lived outside the Walls, but the Titans never so much as looked at them. They didn't munch on grass, either. This meant that they only had an appetite for humans, but that posed its own set of questions. In the end, the only thing he learned was the extent of his own ignorance.

"I guess I have to go outside, after all."

Realizing that he was back where he started, Angel put his hand to his forehead and groaned.

"Xenophon might have been right."

In other words, focus on development and wait for their chance.

Reconstruction of the town was proceeding at a clip, and if he focused on his work, time would pass by in a flash. As long as he didn't let any opportunities go to waste, he would surely be able to speak to the commander some day. It may have been wishful thinking, but he couldn't bear to look at the situation any other way.

***

Angel was summoned by Caspar while he was diligently working on upgrading the Equipment.

"What's it going to be this time…"

Angel scowled as he stood in front of the chief's office. Nothing good had ever come from being summoned by Caspar. It meant that one of two things was going to happen: he would be scolded, or a random task was going to be forced on him. The worst of all possibilities, being scolded and then being given extra work, was plausible, too.

His memories fresh, Angel's spirits sagged, but he also realized that just worrying would accomplish nothing. He scratched his head and opened the door to the chief's office before his mood could sour.

"Ah, you're finally here!"

Caspar stayed flopped atop his sofa as he beckoned Angel in. In addition to Caspar, a soldier whom Angel recognized was inside the room.

"I don't think I need to introduce you. Ya know him, right?"

Caspar meant to skip a full introduction. Indeed, there was no need for one.

"Jorge Piquer. The commander of the Survey Corps, right? What's he doing here?"

"What's he doing here? You're the one who summoned him."

"Me? I'd never—" *do such a thing,* Angel was on the verge of protesting.

He realized, however, that in fact he had.

"So now you come…"

"Please, don't hold it against me. Your proposal touches on a delicate subject. You understand, don't you?"

Jorge stared at Angel with his sharp, chiseled face. His glare was like a sharpened blade, and his beard accentuated his rugged aura. The man exuded an overwhelming presence, and even a feral beast might have turned tail and run if he so much as glared at it.

"If you've come to meet me, that must mean the situation has changed."

Jorge's excuse struck Angel as self-serving, but he kept himself from saying anything more. The commander of the Survey Corps, of all people, had come himself to visit him. Something critical must have happened. Something the Survey Corps found inconvenient.

Quite convenient for me, though.

With less negotiating to do, he expected their conversation to proceed briskly.

"A change in the political landscape, or what have you," Caspar motioned.

"Caused by the earlier Titan attack. I'm sure you've heard talk about the Survey Corps being dissolved?"

"Plenty of times."

Jorge responded to Angel's immediate answer with a bitter laugh. "Well, it's probably more than just a rumor this time. Dissolution is a real possibility."

"The Titans scared the residents stiff. They're saying that opening the gates again would be nuts," elaborated Caspar.

"And why the hell wouldn't they, after actually seeing one of those monsters?"

"I regret what happened to them on our watch. To your colleague, too."

Caspar must have told him about Corina. Jorge lowered his head and apologized.

That's surprising.

Angel appreciated Jorge's reaction. The commander of the Survey Corps, a symbol of power, had unhesitatingly apologized. It wasn't an easy thing to do. It showed his mettle, and Angel could see why soldiers put their lives in his hands as they left to go beyond the gates, a place only steps removed from death.

"The conservatives are riding on public opinion to increase their influence. That means we don't have much time."

"Those bastards might even seal the gates," Caspar added.

"Which would naturally lead to the dissolution of the Survey Corps, huh? I don't know if I should call that underhanded, or just standard procedure for those shut-ins."

"A rise in the conservatives' power is bad news for our workshop, too. We and the corps have a give-and-take relationship. You know how it works."

"It'd probably put a lot of people out of jobs. Including me."

The biggest problem, though, wasn't a decrease in orders or the loss of jobs. It was that they would lose chances to advance technology. The arms the craftsmen made may have been designed to effectively kill enemies, but there were also many essential household items that came about as a result of their work. A portable gas stove using Iceburst Stone was a case in point.

"In other words, you want to shut the conservatives up."

"I can't say it in too loud a voice, but yes." Jorge nodded with a solemn expression, then continued, "What we need is a present that can do just that."

"A Titan head."

"Prove that the Titans can be killed and he can shut those bastards up."

"That's not all. It would allow the people to live in peace again, and even give us hope for our prospects outside the Walls."

Jorge was thinking about more than what would happen to the Survey Corps, about the future of humanity. Everything down to their aspirations was different between the Survey Corpsmen who risked their lives on the front lines and the politicians who sat back in the interior as they squabbled over power. While Angel had already made up his mind, his resolve only grew stronger upon learning how Jorge felt.

"We should be able to defeat the Titans. I don't have proof, but it has to be possible," Angel asserted.

"Anything that's alive can be killed, yes?" Jorge said pensively. "I understand you've been investigating the Titans on your own. Have you

110

found any leads?"

"Wuh?!" Angel's voice cracked in response to Jorge's surprise attack.

"Don't tell me you thought you hadn't been noticed," mocked Caspar.

"Er, well, that's…" Angel stammered.

"I'll admit that we made mistakes, and it's true that it caused countless deaths and injuries, but we're not incompetent."

"I, um… I'm sorry."

"I don't mean to take you to task."

"Hey, if they were going to do something to you, you'd already be arrested, don'cha think?"

Angel grumbled in powerless frustration at Caspar's point.

"What I'd like to do is share information and work together with you to deal with the Titans. What do you say?"

"That's exactly what I want. In fact, that was my proposal, originally. But I don't have any information of real value. You people probably know more than I do, right?"

Angel conveyed what he had learned about the Titans from the Wall, but most of the information was on external traits.

"The investigation into the Titans has only begun. We're sure to find something that will lead us to their weakness eventually."

"I guess my butt's out of there in any case."

"What a load of bull. You're just getting started!"

Caspar's angry voice instinctively made Angel duck.

"As the survey proceeds, we'll need arms made to target the Titans' weaknesses."

"We'll get more orders and rake in the dough!"

"Not like a cent of that will be going to my wallet," Angel snorted. "But how are you going to study the Titans?"

"That's where you play a role, you see. Already coming in handy."

"We might be 'studying' them, but there's only one thing we want to know."

"If you can kill them, right?"

"Exactly." Jorge nodded solemnly. "Our mission will be to discover their weak spots and to learn how much we need to hurt them before they die."

"Animal testing, so to speak?"

"Fortunately, we only need one test subject."

"Just one?"

"As you know, Titans possess incredible recuperative abilities. They regenerate limbs like a lizard regrows its tail, and in a matter of minutes."

"There we go, they might be fearsome monsters, but they also make great test subjects."

"So we slice one up until it dies?"

Titans could lose all four limbs and regenerate them in minutes. Not only did this make them excellent test subjects, it meant that just one would do.

"I don't think they'll make it easy for us to conduct tests on them, though."

"Don't be daft. That's why they need you to make them something."

"We want you to develop equipment that will allow us to capture a Titan."

"Equipment to capture a Titan… Like a net?" It would require something strong enough to capture a Titan and immobilize it. "That's a tough one right off the bat."

"What, giving up before you even try?"

"As if," Angel shot back.

Still, it would take him more than a day or two to create a net for capture, especially after he had seen how absurdly powerful the Titans were.

"When do you plan to go on your next expedition?"

"A month from now."

"That's pretty soon."

"You heard him. That means they'll need the capture net by then."

"It's already hard enough in this atmosphere to go on an expedition. The next one might be our last."

"So failure is not an option…" Angel began to feel nervous all of a sudden, but as a craftsman, he couldn't allow himself to retreat.

This might be the fork in the road.

Live humbly as caged birds, or fly out, knowing the trouble in store? If they chose the former, humanity would peacefully decline in exchange for distance from the Titans. The latter was a thorny path, but it meant that the human species would retain a glimmer of hope.

So it's all up to whether we can defeat a Titan or not.

Not only that, their success rode on the net Angel himself would be making. No wonder he was feeling nervous. His body shook.

"Just wet yourself?" Caspar teased.

"I'm trembling with excitement," Angel replied with a nonplussed expression and began thinking about his capture net.

***

"You need to thank me." Those were the words Xenophon uttered upon entering Angel's lab, and the guy wasn't even sleepwalking.

Angel let out an obvious sigh. He didn't have time to deal with Xenophon.

The capture net completely occupied Angel's mind. While it would be easy enough to produce one by basing the design on a standard casting net, the problem was the net's strength. He had thought of weaving together the wires used in his Equipment, but he had already proven himself that there were issues with their durability. It was doubtful that they could keep a Titan from budging.

"If you don't have a reason to be here, get out."

"What a way to greet someone. Especially when he's brought you something useful."

"Useful?" Angel tilted his head and looked at Xenophon.

"You were looking for material for your net, weren't you?"

"Why do you…"

"I've received a request, too." Xenophon proudly lifted his beloved blade, a smile creeping onto his mouth. "I'm to prepare short swords to be equipped by the Survey Corps."

"Ready for the kill, huh?"

"Would you want it any other way?"

"Fair enough," Angel nodded. "Say, you just said something interesting. About materials."

"If you want to capture a Titan, you need a net that's tough enough to do the job. Right?"

"You have one?"

"I do," Xenophon said so casually that Angel was almost disappointed. "I think you know about this material, too."

"I do?"

Angel furrowed his brow, then immediately started searching around his brain. If Xenophon was right, Angel might as well have proclaimed himself an idiot. It would be an embarrassment to him as a craftsman, and Xenophon may have realized this in keeping himself from giving the answer.

Angel tugged at various threads of memories.

Threads...

Just when he thought he'd distracted himself, it came to him. "Oh. Threads."

"Correct." Xenophon whistled and brought an Iron Bamboo leaf out from his breast pocket.

"You mean spinning the leaf fibers into yarn and making a net from that."

"It may be a leaf, but it's still Iron Bamboo tough. I think it'll make a strong net."

Iron Bamboo's strength as a material had already been proven. A capture net made from its fibers could be the ultimate kind.

"All right, please get ready to depart."

"Depart?"

"To fell Iron Bamboo. We need material before we can get started, don't we?"

A huge number of leaves would be needed to make a net. Xenophon would need to collect a significant amount of Iron Bamboo to produce his short swords, too. They would be procuring their materials from the same source, so Xenophon must have thought that it would be more efficient to work together.

"I've made arrangements to go to the factory city. Let's hurry up and get ready and get going!" Xenophon chirped and swiftly exited the development lab.

Given the man's mood, he might start hunting for bamboo shoots in addition to procuring the needed materials.

With an appalled *sheesh*, Angel went back to thinking about the details of his capture net.

***

The Iron Bamboo grew in a mountainous area on the north side of the factory city. The unexplored area, located close to Wall Sheena, was extremely forbidding with not so much as a path leading through it. The most that existed was an animal trail, but it was difficult to tread, with thick foliage obstructing one's view. No one would visit the area by choice, and that was precisely why the Iron Bamboo had been undiscovered for so long.

"Hard work like this must be a completely foreign concept to the people of Wall Sheena," Xenophon said, parting grass with his hands as if he were swimming.

"Yeah, it's full of privileged folks, beginning with the royalty."

Other people who lived there included those wealthy enough to pay up to acquire citizenship within Wall Sheena. While that was beyond regular folks, it was also possible to earn citizenship there by contributing to the country. The fastest way was to become a decorated soldier. It was the only way to escape poverty and meant an endless source of men and women who wanted to join the corps.

"I wish I was born into royalty, too," quipped Xenophon.

"You wouldn't have any freedom to speak of."

"You wouldn't have a worry in the world either, though."

"What if you got involved in a political struggle and were assassinated?" The conservatives and reformers were indeed involved in political strife, and nothing good could come of getting entangled in it. "A craftsman's life isn't so bad. And if it's Wall Sheena citizenship that you care so much about, you might get it as a reward if we can really bring down a Titan."

"I see. We'll go with that, then."

"We? Count me out."

While they were busy bantering, a bamboo thicket came into sight. The silvery-white bamboo was Iron Bamboo, and its wild growth gave the area a chilly feel as if it had snowed there.

"Iron Bamboo may have originally been no different from regular bamboo that you'd see in the wild."

Xenophon crouched down and pointed at an Iron Bamboo stem. A close examination revealed variations in thickness and color.

"It seems to take a number of years for these to become what we call Iron Bamboo."

"There could be a rare metal under the ground here."

"Want to just dig those up instead?"

Angel briefly considered Xenophon's suggestion. There was no guarantee that the buried metal would be identical. If Iron Bamboo formed as a result of the plant accumulating various minerals found in the soil, the metals slumbering underground possibly weren't worth much on their own. Angel relayed his thoughts to Xenophon.

"I see. They might lose their value if we dig them up."

"It grows out in bamboo form without our lifting a finger. Saves us the trouble of digging, too."

"All right, then why don't we start harvesting."

Angel and Xenophon grabbed their Iron Bamboo short swords and began chopping down everything in sight.

***

A significant amount of Iron Bamboo was needed in order to supply every member of the Survey Corps with a short sword. The order was for sixty short swords, to be exact, and gathering enough Iron Bamboo to make them left a section of the thicket bare. It was not as if they had leveled the entire area, only about a tenth of it. But once the value of the material became well-known, it would only be a matter of time before it was cleared. While the thicket would no doubt come under the control of the royal government, rotating the harvest could stabilize the supply. Unlike minerals, there was no danger of permanently exhausting the supply of bamboo, and its vitality made for easy management. It was unclear how many years it took for bamboo to turn into Iron Bamboo, but they would learn that in time, too.

The capture net and the short swords were manufactured in the factory city. The workshops there banded together to create the swords under Xenophon's supervision, while Angel alone undertook the production of the capture net. It was a matter of repeating simple tasks over and over. Heat Iron Bamboo leaves and strip them to their fibers, spin them into threads, then twine them into rope. He would then weave those together to create a net. The work was straightforward, which was why it required persistence.

Their work in the factory city eventually came to an end, and they returned to Shiganshina District two days before the expedition.

***

The pub was bustling with activity. It was still bright outside, with some time until sunset, but fifty or so people had packed the establishment to capacity. It was so full of the smell of liquor and tobacco that the scent alone seemed enough to intoxicate you. Half of the customers, in fact, were in high spirits, talking cheerfully about this or that building being rebuilt today and who had been discharged from the hospital the other day. Surprisingly, talk of the Survey Corps' expedition was among their heartening topics. Of course, they were less interested in the expedition's results than the celebratory parade to come.

In any case, the strong mood of self-restraint imposed after the Titan attack had started to relax, and the town was regaining its vitality. It would still take time for psychological wounds to heal and to become nothing more than memories, but the signs were good.

"So, here are the fruits of our labor."

Angel placed a short sword made from Iron Bamboo on the table. Receiving it was Solm, who sat on the other side of the table, Maria next to him.

"We were short-handed, so I sharpened it myself. You're welcome."

"Let's see how blunt it is," Solm baited Angel. He unsheathed the short sword and checked its blade. "It seems to at least have something resembling a cutting edge."

"Give it back if you don't want it."

"No, I'll gratefully accept this." Solm sheathed the blade and tucked it away. "That look in your eyes seemed a lot sharper, though."

Angel chuckled at this and reached for a brimming glass of wine on the table.

"How did the capture net go?" inquired Maria.

"I think I'm starting to develop an interest in sewing."

"Good to hear." Maria grinned, but her smile quickly disappeared. "Is it true that you're going to join the expedition?"

"Yeah."

"I think it's too dangerous."

"That's why Solm will be there. He'll risk his life to protect mine."

Angel had decided to come along on the expedition so he could note the Titans' weaknesses and use the information to develop new arms. The unexpected could always happen outside the Walls, but they would gain nothing by being timid. This was something he needed to do in order to free mankind from its fear of the Titans.

"Seems like Xenophon got cold feet." Solm smirked and tossed down a drink.

"I tried inviting him, but he said no. I can't believe he'd let this opportunity go to waste."

"I think it's a sensible decision," Maria countered.

"Yeah, being attacked by a Titan once is enough…"

Picturing a Titan was enough to send shivers through Angel's body, but he was not going on the expedition to be killed. He was going out there to kill a Titan instead. It wouldn't do to be scared.

"If you'll allow me to change topics," Solm said in a formal tone, "I've actually submitted a reassignment request."

"A reassignment request?"

"The next expedition will be my last. After it, I'll be leaving the Survey Corps."

"Do you mind if I ask why?"

Solm nodded at Angel's question. "I believe that the Survey Corps will return from the next expedition with significant results."

"We're going to upend common sense, after all."

"I've always wanted to obtain some sort of result. And to stay where I was until I did."

"And defeating a Titan would mean just that."

"Yes."

"So you'll be transferring into the Garrison? I guess you could be an instructor for trainees, too. Or how about you get Wall Sheena citizenship and live the high life?"

"It's too early for me to retire. I intend to protect the town as a member of the Garrison."

"So do you feel better now, Maria?"

Angel looked over at her, but she looked concerned rather than relieved.

"Is something the matter?" he asked.

"Of course! You still have the expedition ahead of you!" she exclaimed, then let out a big sigh. "Solm going on an expedition is enough to make my stomach hurt, but now you say you're going with him. What're you going to do if this ends up affecting the baby?"

"The baby? Wait—"

Angel looked back and forth between Solm and Maria.

"Really?!"

"Apparently so."

"It hasn't sunk in yet, though."

The two seemed a little apprehensive, but their radiant smiles made it clear they were both more happy than anything.

"Wow. You're going to be parents…"

The news of their child was a bundle of joy for Angel too. Since Solm and Maria were like family to him, it was as if his own family were about to gain a new member, and it moved him all the more.

Two people who never knew their parents becoming parents themselves. I bet they'll dote on the kid.

The child would surely be spared any of the sadness they themselves might have felt during their early years.

"If we're going to be parents, that means you're going to be an uncle."

"I think you mean a big brother," Angel replied in a flash, raising his hand and calling out to a waiter. "We'll have an advance celebration tonight. Let's drink!"

"Now that's a good idea."

"Hey! You better not let it affect the expedition," Maria warned in a resigned tone.

***

The light of dawn illuminated the darkness then swiftly banished it, bringing color to the hazy town. There were a few clouds, but the weather was excellent. The clear blue sky promised a halcyon day.

Still, the early morning air was piercing cold. It was enough to chill you down to the bone even with a cloak and hood on. While Angel cursed his weakly body, the soldiers seemed not to notice the cold, facing forward in formation and standing absolutely still even though they wore the same outfit that he did. An armor called muscles must have been blocking out the cold.

At the front of the formation were Jorge, the commander, and two deputy commanders. Behind them were Teams 1 through 5, each led by a team leader. A group of sixty. Angel would join Team 3, located in the center of the formation and temporarily led by Solm.

Throughout the Survey Corps' history, it was extremely rare for anyone unaffiliated with the group to participate in an expedition. The corps normally consisted of ten Teams, but having suffered large losses in the last expedition, and unable to replenish their ranks in the turmoil that followed the Titan invasion, they'd been forced to reorganize. It was a fairly unique situation, but the soldiers did not seem nerved up. Their daily training had tempered their iron wills to handle the most difficult circumstances.

It was the best and strongest lineup that one could wish for, but Angel felt unease welling up inside of him, and he trembled.

"I thought I told you to use the toilet first," Solm cajoled. "It's not too late to pull out. What'll you do?"

"Don't be stupid."

"All right, then," Solm laughed, leisurely looking to the sky.

Angel found himself looking up with him. It had grown much brighter while they were chatting about nothing. When he looked toward the front of the formation, Jorge had his right arm raised high.

"We're moving out!"

At the command, the giant gate slowly started to open, showing them a desolate, uninhabited plain.

The Survey Corps began to advance as the gate opened.

His tension skyrocketing, Angel's heart started racing in his chest. His body seemed to be out of balance and an awful sweat poured out of him from head to toe.

"All right, let's go take a gander at some Titans."

Solm smacked Angel hard on the shoulder and let his horse trot ahead.

The numbing blow returned Angel to his senses. He slapped both of his cheeks to regain his nerve.

"Muscle head…" he grimaced and hastily spurred on his mount.

***

The Survey Corps streaked southward down their trackless path. The sun shone higher two hours after they had left Shiganshina District. The edge had been taken off of the cold air, but the scenery had not changed much. More trees were visible, but there were few other differences. They found no traces of civilization such as the ruins of towns or villages, and spotted nothing but animals. They had yet to find their target, a Titan, either.

We've come pretty far out.

Angel looked behind him on his cantering mount. Since they were around ten kilometers from Shiganshina, Wall Maria was now only dimly visible.

If we were to be attacked by Titans here…

Angel's body instinctively shrank. Even their trained group of cavalry would never cover ten kilometers in a flash. At full speed, it would still take ten minutes or so.

Surveying his surroundings anew, Angel could tell just how expansive the outside world was. No matter which way he looked, he saw a flat horizon. It gave him an overwhelming sense of freedom, but he also felt unease. Although they were a large group, he felt isolated as if he'd lost his way in an unknown land.

"The orphanage director told me something when I was a child," Solm spoke, looking straight forward while riding by Angel's side. "They say most of the world is covered by waters called the Sea."

"The Sea?"

"Of course, I don't know if he'd actually seen it, or if he had just learned about it in a book."

"For all that Sea or whatever's out there, I don't see so much as a puddle around us." Angel made a show of looking around.

"In other words, we haven't even reached this Sea yet."

"Which means the world…"

"Is unfathomably large."

That would make sense of the endless wasteland. It may have seemed unfathomably broad to human senses, but perhaps it wasn't all that from a different perspective.

"This Sea could be right ahead of us."

Just as Angel strained his eyes, he heard the pop of something like an explosion. A deep-red smoke signal bloomed like a rose in the south sky.

Tension spread through the soldiers when they confirmed it. A Red

Star from a flare gun had exploded overhead, signaling that Team 1, who were acting as advance scouts, had found one Titan. A Yellow Star followed it.

They're bringing a Titan back with them.

The combination of the Red Star and the Yellow Star conveyed Team 1's message. While signal flares could alert any Titans in the vicinity, the creatures had the odd trait of not reacting to sound despite having ears.

After a moment, a Red Star and five Yellow Stars bloomed in the air.

So the Titan is about five meters tall.

Angel brought his hand to his chest and forced himself to exhale deeply. He could feel through his palm that his heart was beating significantly faster.

It's okay. This is the plan.

They were on the expedition to capture and to examine the behavior of a Titan. Multiple Red Stars would have gone up if there had been more than one Titan, in which case they would be playing it safe and retreating.

The plan's going forward, then.

A cold sweat began to rise from Angel's pores.

"All troops, assume your positions!"

Teams 2 through 5 created a V-shaped formation on Jorge's order. At the center of the formation was Jorge, the commander, and his two deputy commanders were placed at each wing. As Angel would be useless in a fight and potentially disrupt the formation, he would steer clear of the operation, simply observing from behind.

Angel's eyes caught something. "They're here…"

What looked like a cloud emerging in the distance quickly grew in presence. It was a plume of dust. Soon, cavalry, assumably Team 1, appeared to the fore. They grew closer every second, the cloud of dust their horses kicked up in tow.

"Advance!"

The moment Jorge gave the command, the formation moved forward, intact. It almost appeared as though they were going to intercept Team 1, but that was not the case. They had visual confirmation on humanity's nemesis, a Titan, trailing by about three hundred meters. He looked like a young man in his late teens, but his body stood a towering five meters tall. His emaciated body seemed to be nothing but skin and bones, and his face seemed to be on the verge of tears, but he certainly hadn't come seeking to be comforted by the Survey Corps. Flopping his arms back and forth more than appeared necessary, stumbling numerous times, he ran and ran after Team 1, his food.

Team 1 broke to both sides just before reaching the main formation, but the Titan continued to advance, seemingly carried by his momentum. Soldiers on both wings gripped the capture net. On Jorge's command, the wings encircled the Titan, and a moment later, the capture net was cast over his head. The Titan's arms and legs became tangled in the fine mesh, causing him to fall flat on his face.

"Yes!"

Angel finally allowed himself to exhale in relief and quietly pumped his fist. There seemed to be no problems with the net's strength, with no signs that it would tear. The more the Titan struggled, the more he tangled himself into the net. He was eventually wrapped so tight he could no longer move.

"Yeaaah!"

A cheer rose over the soldiers, but the real work was yet to come. The troops formed a circle around the Titan and stood guard. Moving to the center of the formation, Angel dismounted and walked toward the Titan. Jorge and several soldiers followed behind him.

"The more I look at him, the more human he seems."

Aside from his large mouth that stretched from ear to ear, there was practically no difference between the Titan and a human. He was, quite literally, a titanic human. Unlike Mammon he was lean, but appearances could be misleading. He looked emaciated from a lack of nutrition, but that did not necessarily mean he was on the verge of starving to death.

Why does he have to look so human? Look more like a monster, you monster…

No mercy would be shown to a Titan, but the creature's undeniably human appearance made Angel weirdly conscious.

He reached toward the Titan's upper arm.

This is creeping me out…

But he had to touch.

Titans aren't human. They're just monsters.

The best way for Angel to internalize this would be to touch one.

The moment his fingers touched the Titan's skin, he felt out of sorts.

Warm…

Surprisingly, the Titan's body was warm. Because of their cruel habit of eating humans, he'd assumed the Titans would be cold-blooded like reptiles. Yet they seemed to be warm-blooded like humans. Only, the body temperature was higher than a human's, almost hot to the touch.

"Why don't we get started."

Unsheathing their short swords on Jorge's command, the troops on hand placed their blades against both of the Titans knees and sliced. Instead of blood, steam spewed out of his body. Whether it was his blood boiling or some metabolic effect, the result did underwrite a high body temperature.

"Doesn't even make a peep. Either they don't feel pain or they don't have vocal cords," Jorge noted as he watched the soldiers work.

The Titan's weepy face made him look as though he were in pain, but since the creatures' expressions never changed, it was impossible to judge what emotion he was exhibiting.

The soldiers silently continued their work. The Iron Bamboo short swords worked on the Titan, but not well enough to cut cleanly through. His skin gave way but snapping bone was an arduous task; the soldiers were drenched in sweat and breathing heavily by the time they'd finally succeeded. Given how it was even with Iron Bamboo, blades made out of mere steel not standing a chance made sense. The cross-section showed bone, vessels, muscles, and such as one might expect to see on a human. While they were not medical experts, taking home a sample would surely advance their knowledge of the Titans. As they tried to pack away the severed leg, however, it disintegrated, steaming, into dust and ashes that were carried off by the wind.

"What's with that…"

Angel tried to understand the phenomenon taking place before his eyes, but he couldn't come up with a convincing explanation. As their sample disappeared, the Titan's leg soon began to regenerate, the wound closing and buds of flesh sprouting as if to scab over it. These swiftly formed into a leg, a complete restoration in just a few minutes. Jorge had previously compared the Titans' recuperative abilities to a lizard regrowing its tail, and now Angel had the same impression. Of course, there was a huge difference in the rate of regeneration.

Are they really an organism?

While monsters did not call for common sense, these Titans were creatures that lived in the same world as Angel.

I suppose they're an organism with astonishing recuperative powers.

Yet he could scarce leave it at that.

Well, mulling over it won't get us anywhere...

They'd learned that the Titans had no weaknesses below their knees. He had to consider it another step toward comprehending the Titans.

Switching gears, Angel took out a handful of bombs from his saddlebag. They contained enough firepower to stock a small ammunition dump. Xenophon had enthusiastically prepared a variety of explosives for him.

"Severing limbs takes too long. Let's optimize."

Setting the explosives on the Titan's arms and legs, Angel summarily detonated them. The Titan's limbs flew off, but most of the chunks of flesh were contained thanks to the net. Again, the pieces of meat turned to dust, and any missing parts were restored in moments. A human would have expired from massive blood loss, but there were no signs of that happening to the Titan.

They moved to blowing up the lower abdomen, and upon inspection, failed to note any reproductive organs.

"Do Titans have genders?"

There was the possibility that the Titan was female despite looking outwardly male. Although hermaphroditism was not out of the question, how they would breed without reproductive organs was a mystery.

Do they not need to reproduce? Don't tell me they divide.

But the Titans embodied irrationality. A full body regenerating from a severed arm or leg wouldn't be all that much more bizarre.

I hope not, though…

The nightmarish scenario gave Angel goose bumps, but he quickly shook his head, collected himself, and proceeded to destroy the Titan's abdomen. With an explosion it ruptured, and entrails gleaming pink poured out. Still, the creature's vitality showed no sign of abating.

I can't believe this bastard.

The Titan's body lost no time regenerating before a dumbfounded Angel.

Could they really be immortal?

Angel drew the short sword at his waist and thrust it into the Titan's chest. Its tip piercing skin and crunching bone, the blade plunged in to the hilt. The sword should have skewered the Titan's heart, but breathing his last seemed far from his mind.

"Damn it!" Angel spat, and walked toward the head.

Despite being pinned down, upon noticing Angel, the Titan opened his mouth wide. An eloquent statement: no thunderous loss of limb, no blade sticking out of the chest merited any attention, but as long as he could move he would go on eating, and eating. The absurd response half-appalled, half-intimidated Angel.

"Please, just die."

Angel stared into the dark abyss that was the Titan's mouth and tossed explosives inside. Moments later, the Titan's head exploded, his cranium flying in what looked like a volcanic eruption. The flesh on his face had peeled back, leaving behind a few writhing and twitching mimetic muscles. Even if the Titan wanted to curse Angel, most of his face had been scattered about and not a trace of his features remained. The shock of the explosion seemed to have shaken the brain apart; it oozed out of the cracked head in a soupy state. It was too harrowing a spectacle to look straight upon. Still, Angel could not feel pity for the Titan.

Compared to what Corina…what all the humans you monsters ate suffered, this is nothing.

Corina's figure after Mammon's blow had turned her into a lump of meat was still fresh in Angel's mind. Nothing would ever ease the chagrin of the dead or the sorrow of the deceased's loved ones.

The Titans were atrocious. Zeroing in on their regenerative abilities and destroying a Titan's body over and over, however, was no less diabolical.

Maybe I won't be dying peacefully in bed, either...

If so, there was no point in showing mercy at this stage. There was no choice but to mute his emotions and harden his heart.

Perhaps destroying the head had worked, and the Titan was limp.

"Did we get it?"

They couldn't be certain, not knowing how to define death in this case. Measuring a human's pulse told you if the fellow was alive or dead, but it was unthinkable that the method worked on a Titan.

Unthinkable...

Angel reached his hand out toward the Titan's neck.

If there's no pulse... If this guy doesn't start moving...

Then perhaps that signified the death of a Titan. Still, Angel had his doubts, and the uncertainty would linger until all traces of the Titan's body disappeared from existence.

Maybe we should just blow the body to smithereens.

Right as Angel entertained this ruthless idea, a shout came from among the soldiers who had been training their eyes southward.

"Enemy attack!"

From the troops watching the west too came a bellowed warning.

"Enemy attack!!"

The report quickly spread through the formation and riled it up.

"Now of all times..."

The investigation was incomplete, and a load of points still required confirmation. Angel couldn't leave without ascertaining them.

"Prepare to retreat!" commanded Jorge, quickly straddling his horse.

But Angel hesitated. He at least wanted to make sure the Titan was dead.

"We'll save it for another day."

"But there might not be a next time."

"Suffering losses here will have a far bigger effect on any subsequent expedition. Wouldn't you agree?"

Despite the tense circumstances, Jorge, calm and collected, showed sound judgment. After all, they were talking about monsters believed for over a quarter of a century now to be immortal. Trying to off it in the next couple of dozen minutes was a ridiculous idea. As Jorge proposed, it was best to try again another day.

Or as many times as it takes.

Angel consented, glanced at the Titan, then mounted his steed.

The question is what kind of shape this guy will be in when we do come back.

If the Titan was decaying, it would be safe to say that they'd killed him.

But if he's still alive…

Then that's that, Angel persuaded himself. If he managed to do so fairly easily, it was because he saw how humanity might be freed from its birdcage.

If we can't kill them, we can just tie them up.

The total number of Titans in existence was unknown, but if they steadily captured one at a time with nets, they could eventually rid themselves of them.

It'll take time, but it's a possibility.

The soldiers broke their circular formation and began to regroup in the same column formation they'd left in. But when Angel rode toward them to join it, he heard something from behind him. It was the snapping sound of threads being torn apart.

The moment he turned to look at the sound, his eyes opened wide in surprise. The Titan's thin, branch-like arms were jutting out of the ripped capture net.

"Agh…the explosions weakened it."

A durability issue had come to light, while the Titan's body, on which they'd done such a number, was restored with no apparent loss of vitality. Sundering the net to pieces, the Titan, freed of bondage, entered into a mad dash.

"The bastard…"

Paying no mind to the boggled Angel, the Titan assaulted the formation's flank. No doubt having opted for the larger concentration of prey, the creature nevertheless stumbled and fell, sending up a fantastic cloud of dirt. Mounts neighed and reared, and a few riders, shaken off of their horses, tumbled to the ground.

The prone Titan sluggishly raised his upper body. An unlucky soldier who happened to come underneath one of the hands clenching the ground let out an agonized shriek. Grabbing the writhing man's head with his fingers, the Titan slowly pulled it upward. Perhaps having pinched too hard, he crushed the skull of the soldier who was now completely devoid of life, motionless after a few last twitches, blood dripping from dangling arms and legs. Opening a large mouth that stretched from one ear to the other, the Titan started devouring the soldier's body. The terrible sound of snapping bones filled the air.

"Angel! Behind you!!" Solm shouted.

Uh oh…

Angel shuddered at the footfalls approaching unexpectedly from behind. He didn't need to turn around. He could guess what was closing in on him. Distracted by the Titan in front of him, he hadn't noticed what had drawn near.

Whether it was munching or a smacking of lips, the slurping sound offended his ears. Angel was nothing more than prey. He felt an urge to check out his adversary, but there was no time for that. He needed to act and didn't have a second to lose.

He kicked his horse's belly, abruptly setting forth. A sound like a bestial roar arose behind him. A draft of hot putrid breath licked the nape of his neck.

It's over…

Right as Angel had accepted his fate, the sound of a blast surged past him from the front. Not a moment later, he heard a whizzing pass by his ears, then something behind him falling.

"Hurry!"

He looked ahead of him to find Solm aiming a carbine.

Angel coaxed his horse to go faster. He then looked behind, to where a three-meter-class Titan with an air hole between his eyes lay supine on the ground.

Phew…

He was only relieved for a moment, though, as a familiar Titan came charging from the south.

"Mammon—"

Flabby limbs and body jiggling up and down, closing in at a speed belying such a figure, was the same Titan that had barged into Shiganshina District and that had eaten Corina. The Titan with the middle-aged appearance still wore the same beaming smile as he rushed toward them with outstretched arms. Thundering booms reverberated with every step he took, and with them came impressive clouds of dirt.

"Aghh…" Angel let out an indistinct scream.

No human could withstand the embrace of a monstrosity that boasted a height reaching ten meters. There was nothing to do but to urgently turn tail and flee.

"Disperse and withdraw!"

So commanded Jorge, but the Titan was rushing in on them with every moment. The soldiers tried to spur their horses in accordance with Jorge's order, but a number of the steeds were past control, terrified as they must have been by a Titan accompanied by earth tremors. Meanwhile the Titan arrived, and picked a prey close by.

"Ah, aaaaagh!" a member of the Survey Corps, renowned for its ferocity, let out a pitiful scream.

The Titan raised his blubbery right arm above his head and flattened the man with his palm.

"Humans…aren't bugs…"

Pinching the soldier's head, the Titan carried it to his maw. He wriggled his mouth as if to savor the taste and, skillfully removing just the head, tossed it on the ground. The freshly-severed head covered in saliva tumbled across the earth, its grimy face wearing a clear expression of terror.

"You think you can do whatever you want…"

But the circumstances ruled out any attempt at revenge, and it wasn't such an impulse that visited Angel.

Reaching out for more food, the Titan snatched another soldier as casually as if he were picking a berry he'd spotted on the roadside, and proceeded to stuff his cheeks.

"Damned monster!" a soldier yelled, firing a carbine at the Titan.

"You idiot! Just run!!" screamed Angel, but his words didn't reach the soldier.

Witnessing a comrade's grisly end seemed to have sapped his alertness. Tossing his gun away, he grabbed the short sword on his hip and charged cursing toward the Titan.

"Don't bother… Let's go!" Solm urged, biting his lip, his slightly trembling finger pointed north.

Angel nodded, kicked his horse, and took flight. The surviving soldiers also began to retreat with Jorge in the lead. They could hear agonizing screams coming from behind them.

Damn it… Damn it!

Angel cursed in his heart but didn't look back. He faced forward and rode on. If he mustered up some small amount of courage and confronted the Titans, he'd die like a dog. They needed to advance as far as they could while the Titans toyed with the soldiers.

I'm sorry…

All Angel could do was make sure the soldiers' death wouldn't be in vain.

The tide of the battle couldn't turn any worse. In fact, calling it a battle was too generous. It was a one-sided massacre by the Titans.

That was not the only tragedy they faced, either. The three-meter-class Titan had already recovered, and they could see him charging in from ahead. Angel and Solm attempted to evade him by splitting to both sides, and the Titan's momentum carried him through the gap. Since shrieks arose behind them, the troops following after them must have fallen victim instead. It was as clear as day that a hellish scene was unfolding.

Escape. That's all I can do…

They were up against unfathomable monsters that brushed off even the strongest equipment they could prepare. Trying to fight the Titans was foolish. Their confidence had been ground to dust, and their bodies and minds felt withered.

They were about ten kilometers away from Shiganshina District. Barring further trouble, it would take ten minutes to get there. But the footfalls rushing in from behind quite clearly told them how unlikely that was.

Hurry, please!

Angel whipped his horse. He couldn't afford to tarry a single second. If the Titans got him, it was all over. Begging for mercy meant nothing to monsters who didn't understand language, and sobbing and crying would have no effect, either. The Titans would greedily devour him, gulping him down until nothing was left.

Angel's face contorted when he imagined the scene. He timidly turned around. What he saw were three Titans chasing after the fleeing party. Mammon, initially in the rear, brushed aside the two Titans running ahead of him, spread out his arms, and thundered forth. He must have wanted all the prey for himself. An embodiment of greed. The nightmare in the flesh wore an expression of supreme bliss better suited to an innocent babe.

Hurry... Faster...

The Titan was about three hundred meters away. It was a considerable distance but failed to put Angel at ease. The footfalls felt close, and the intent to do harm searing. Although Jorge was still present, the Survey Corps had already been partially wiped out.

Do we slip through the gate first, or...

The Titan was closing in steadily. The horses continued to gallop but were gradually losing speed. No matter how well-trained, they had a limited supply of stamina.

While the Titan...

Angel wondered but immediately cast his thoughts aside.

For now focus on getting away!

He glared straight ahead to find Wall Maria in the distance. It was about eight kilometers away, but the span seemed like eternity to him.

Jorge, leading the troop, raised his flare gun and fired it. The Black Star that exploded overhead polluted the sky with lurid black smoke. It was a signal to the Garrison soldiers who stood on Wall Maria's watchtower: "Emergency."

We just need to get him in range of the cannons...

That might not fell the Titan, but it could at least stall him. The only problem was that the cannons had a range of two kilometers.

Wall Maria steadily neared, but Angel's mount was on the verge of giving in. Wheezing with every unreliable breath, ready to collapse at any moment, it was slowing down as well.

Angel whipped his horse but barely picked up any speed.

The footfalls had closed in and were now directly behind. A giant man-shaped shadow covered Angel's.

Shit... This is it...

Right as he had started to abandon hope, Solm, who rode beside him, pulled his short sword from its scabbard.

"Hey, what are you—"

Before Angel could finish, Solm had spun his horse around and was charging toward the Titan.

"W-Wait!"

As Angel turned around, bewildered, he saw Solm slashing at the Titan's right knee. The gaping wound was so deep it exposed bone but did not make the Titan fall over, only throwing him off balance. Still, robbed of momentum, he fell to one knee.

Solm seemed to take this as a good opportunity and rode around the Titan on his horse, slashing at the creature with his blade. Moments later, the lower half of the Titan's body was covered in sword wounds.

Solm moved shockingly well, but the Titan still retained his smile, showing no signs of enduring any pain. The wounds began to heal shortly, the erupting steam shrouding his body.

Still not enough for a Titan...

Solm should have known this, too, but the Corpsman nevertheless continued to swing his sword. The Titan, denied the time to recuperate,

135

continued to spew hot smoke in the place of fresh blood.

Even the mighty Titan must have found Solm annoying as he leapt around like a gnat. He flailed his giant, trunk-like arms about, and while the ill-aimed sweeps failed to snag Solm, a direct hit would mean certain and immediate death. It was a chilling sight, but Solm was the superior fighter.

Solm's stalling tactics allowed the soldiers in front to put a considerable amount of distance between the Titan and themselves. At this rate, the Titan would be within cannon range before he caught up to them. Fortunately, the other Titans were lagging behind. Possibly not as interested in live prey as Mammon, the three-meter-class was occupied with corpses nearer on hand, while the lanky one was so busy stumbling he would never catch up with them.

Apparently satisfied with his results, Solm disengaged and made to retreat.

"Solm! Hurry!!" Angel screamed.

The Corpsman set his horse running, but one of the Titan's flailing arms grazed his body.

"Ugh…"

Solm's body slammed into the ground hard, bouncing a few times before coming to a rest, bent and writhing. While he did have some luck, in that he survived, his right leg must have snapped and was twisted in an unnatural direction. Considering the situation, it was unlikely that Solm's injuries stopped there.

Angel leapt forward on his horse, hurrying toward Solm. As expected, the Titan still could not move due to the damage inflicted on his legs, but it was only a matter of time before he would be mobile.

"Solm!" Angel shouted, lowering his right hand and almost grazing the ground while his horse still ran. "Solm! Give me your hand!!"

Solm understood Angel's intention and, despite contorting his face in agony, managed to reach out his hand. Angel grabbed Solm's arm and pulled up with every bit of his strength. He was not quite powerful enough, and the best he could do was drape Solm's body across the back of his saddle.

Angel made another U-turn on his horse and set off for Shiganshina District as fast as he could.

"Are you trying to get yourself killed?!" Angel yelled, criticizing Solm's deed. Then he said, "Just wait, I'll get you to a doctor right now." But the horse was completely exhausted, not to mention overloaded. It was hard to tell if it could even cover the rest of the distance.

"Maria's gonna scold me…"

"And I will too."

"She's scarier than she looks…" Solm snickered.

"Hurry! He's coming!!" Jorge shouted, but the horse had reached its limits long ago.

"Just a little more! C'mon!"

Angel tried to invigorate his horse with his whip, but the beast merely let out pitiful gasps and would not go faster.

He could hear the Titan's footfalls behind him.

"Angel. Do you have…any of Xenophon's toys left?"

"Yeah." Angel felt around in his bag for a few grenades then handed them to Solm without turning around. "Aim carefully. We can get away once we're within the cannons' firing range."

"…I never miss my target." Solm's voice was lifeless, but his words were full of confidence. "Angel…"

"What's wrong? Hurry up."

"Take care of Maria for me."

"Hey, what do you mean by…" Angel suddenly felt Solm disappear, and his horse sped up. "Solm?!"

When Angel turned back, he couldn't believe what he saw. Solm had leapt off the horse. Using his short sword as a cane, he was meeting the incoming Titan head-on.

"No! S-Stop it!!"

Solm's leg was broken, and he seemed to be in no shape to walk, let alone fight. He had no chance of victory.

The Titan immediately reached his hungry fingers toward Solm, who didn't even have the time to resist. He was grabbed and carried toward the Titan's mouth.

But Solm was not going to let himself be eaten without a fight. "Raaahhh!"

Letting out a war cry, Solm sliced horizontally with his short sword and ripped through both of the Titan's eyes. Neither tears nor blood flowed, but the Titan must have been inconvenienced; he let go of Solm and held his face in both hands.

Solm was free again, but rather than flee, he chose to re-engage the Titan. Burying his short sword in the Titan's throat, he used it as a fulcrum to alight on the creature's body. Distracted by his slashed eyes, the Titan paid no attention to Solm, who used his arms and his good left leg to reach the shoulders. He then grabbed the grenades tucked in his breast pocket, immediately pulled the pins, and clung onto the Titan's nape.

"Solm! Don't!!" Angel yelled.

A moment later, the roar of an explosion ripped through the wasteland with a flash. Solm's body scattered into tiny pieces of meat that plopped down on the ground as if to enrich the cracked earth.

"Ahh…" Angel breathed with a half-resigned expression.

He could feel the strength draining from his body. If he were not on horseback, he would have sunk to the ground.

The strike that cost Solm his life had blown apart the Titan's neck. The head, robbed of support, thudded to the ground, the impact of its own weight distorting its shape. The smile still never left the Titan's face.

"Aaaaahhh!"

A bestial scream came from Angel as he whipped his horse. Obeying, it began to move faster, dashing through the wasteland with all of its strength.

"I swear… I swear I'll kill them!" Angel pledged in his heart, looking back to burn the image of his foe into his eyes. Yet, all he could see there was a preposterous amount of steam. He barely made out the giant silhouette of a Titan, but that was all. Soon, even the silhouette became indistinct as it vanished in the wind. Nothing was left. The Titan and its imposing presence had clean disappeared.

"What…just happened?

There was no time to double back. The skinny Titan had resumed his chase with an obsession.

Cannons sounded, far away.

CHAPTER FOUR

Angel was having a dream. A dream of being attacked by a Titan.

He knew that he was dreaming because he saw the same scene every time he went to sleep. A wide expanse of barren, sand-swept land spread before him, and a gigantic man towered overhead. It was Mammon. Angel, try as he might, couldn't forget his fearless smile. Mammon clenched Solm's body with such ease that his best friend might as well have been a doll.

"Again? You're doing this to Solm again?"

Solm's face contorted in agony and blood frothed from his mouth.

"Stop!"

Complaining to a dream was meaningless, but he could not stay silent. He never wanted to see Solm suffering again.

Mammon showed no signs of complying with Angel's request. The Titan squeezed Solm's body like a fresh fruit. All four of Solm's limbs bent in impossible angles as bones jutted out of his torn skin, fresh blood dripping on the ground.

"Aaaaahhh!"

As soon as Angel shrieked clawing at his hair, he was jolted awake by the loudness of his own voice.

"Just…a dream."

But the dream seemed all too real. His heart was ringing like an alarm, and his night sweats were so severe that he was drenched down to his underwear.

Attacked even in my dreams…

Angel took deep breaths to calm his disordered breathing. A week had passed since the expedition, but the persistent nightmares only continued to wear on his body and mind.

So there's nowhere to run.

It was all due to the expedition's disastrous outcome. They had set off enthused to shed light on the Titans' behavior, but merely learned of their enemy's prowess a few times over.

If Solm hadn't held back Mammon, I wouldn't be...

While the task may have been essential to humanity's future, the cost simply had been too large.

If I hadn't joined them on the expedition, he might not have had to die.

He had wondered this countless times since the expedition but always came to the same conclusion.

I bet Solm would say...it's not my fault.

Angel sat up and slapped his cheeks to exhort himself.

"Just gotta move forward," Angel muttered audibly to himself and got out of bed.

As soon as he stood, however, his vision warped like a stick of soft candy. Unable to stay upright, he sank down to the edge of his bed and applied pressure to his temples. He couldn't get enough sleep, nor did he have an appetite, and his body seemed to have grown even weaker than he'd imagined.

While he sighed over his own frailty, there was no time to fuss over it. Solm and Corina would laugh at him if he let a bit of dizziness put him out of action.

What drove Angel, though, was more than just thoughts of his friends but a sense of duty.

"I have to do this."

He grit his teeth and stood up, quickly got dressed, and set off for the lab.

***

"Sheesh, just look at you."

Angel was needled the moment he stepped into the chief's office. The inconsiderate remark came from Caspar, the master of the room. He sat reclined on his sofa and gazed at Angel with an appraising look.

"You look like you're about to collapse. Have you been eating?"

144

"Treated to that scene, not really…"

Every time he slept, the despair he experienced on the expedition revived all over again. It was no wonder that he had no appetite.

"Forget about me, how are things going?"

"That the only thing you care about?" Caspar sighed. "No news," he stated flatly.

While that was enough to discourage Angel, he didn't give up. "Could you try talking to Jorge again? It's important."

"The result's going to be the same no matter how many times I try."

"Dammit." Angel bit his lip. "One more time… I need to go on one more expedition…"

"To do what?"

"To show that we can kill the Titans." It would not have been an overstatement to say that Angel now lived for no other reason than to prove this. "I saw it for myself. A Titan died."

The image was still fresh in his mind. Solm's suicidal attack against Mammon had more than just stalled the creature.

After that, the Titan turned to smoke and disappeared.

Though the scene looked nothing like a human's death, Angel considered it the equivalent. It removed the threat posed by a Titan, so putting aside the process, the result was identical.

While still approximate, he'd also located the Titans' weak point. To be certain of it, he had to go on another expedition to confirm his theory, and the Survey Corps' cooperation was essential for that. Angel had tried to approach Jorge through Caspar but had received absolutely no reply.

"The problem here's that you were the only one to see the Titan die."

"You're saying I'm spouting nonsense?"

"That's not it." Caspar rubbed his shaved head, then glanced at Angel. "But it's hard to prove anything if yer the only one who saw it. Right?"

"But I…"

"Yeah, I know. Ya saw him bite it, I know you did." There was no doubt in Caspar's voice. "And just between us—" Caspar leaned forward before continuing with a solemn expression, "Jorge saw something like that, too."

"He did? He saw the Titan die?!"

Angel grew animated at Caspar's words. No matter how convinced that a Titan had died, Angel was the only one making the claim. He had spoken to the soldiers on the expedition, but none of them had seen the Titan's final moments. In fact, some even suggested it might have been a delusion triggered by the extreme circumstances.

But if Jorge could confirm the Titan's death, that would give credibility to Angel's claim.

"Then why won't Jorge send me a reply?"

"He's probably way too busy dealing with the aftermath of the expedition." Caspar shrugged. "You went on it, so you should know. The Survey Corps was halved in number."

The eighty-man Survey Corps now numbered under thirty. Not only was it no time for another expedition, the future of the force was endangered.

"Still, this is the time if we're going to go." Angel wasn't being stubborn simply in order to get his way. He sensed that if he let this chance slip, he would never get another expedition.

It was common knowledge that the Survey Corps had been dealt a devastating blow. Growing ranks of residents were skeptical about the expeditions, possibly because the loss set back reconstruction. This lent influence to the conservatives and might accelerate their efforts to seal the gates and dissolve the Survey Corps. A step needed to be taken before those decisions could be made.

"They probably feel the same way." Caspar scowled with crossed arms. "In any case, there's nothing we can say that'll make a difference. We've just gotta sit here and wait for a reply."

"But…"

"You just keep developing. Even if they do decide to go on an expedition, there's no point unless they can bring some special gear with 'em."

Caspar was absolutely right, and Angel had no choice but to agree.

He had been so caught up in whether there would be another expedition that he'd neglected his work. Knowing the Titans' weakness wouldn't matter if they didn't possess the appropriate gear, whose development was an urgent task, no question about it.

"Your job is to develop arms. Got that? It's not slaughtering Titans. That's Jorge's job."

"I know." Achieving their goal was nigh impossible if Angel stayed flustered and lost sight of things. He'd nearly made a crucial mistake.

"By the way, have you talked to Maria?"

As soon as Angel heard her name, he felt a pricking pain in his chest.

"Eh? So you still haven't talked to her."

"How could I ever face her... Do I tell her I'm alive thanks to Solm?"

Angel had last seen Maria at the soldiers' funeral service three days earlier, though it would be more accurate to say that he'd simply caught sight of her. She looked exhausted and unapproachable. More to the point, Angel didn't have the courage to speak to her.

"Personally, I think it's yer duty to tell her how Solm died."

"Couldn't Jorge..."

"Are you some kinda idiot?!" Caspar snapped. "Just go tell her what you need to. That's an order from your boss."

"Come on..."

"How else is Maria supposed to sort out her feelings? Or you, for that matter?"

Caspar shooed Angel out of the room.

***

Angel stood in front of Wall Maria's main gate, looking up at its towering presence. Though the wall had allowed Mammon to enter, it was as imposing as ever. The bloodstains and guts flung on it washed away, the Wall now majestically presented itself to Angel as if nothing had ever happened.

He hadn't come to the main gate in order to take a look at Wall Maria's condition. He was interested in the watchtower atop it, and specifically, a soldier stationed there: Maria. While he was obeying Caspar, who'd gone so far as to term it an order, it wasn't as if he were there unwillingly. As the one who'd witnessed Solm's final moments and heard his dying request, he certainly felt that he needed to speak to Maria. What he had to say was simply too cruel, however, and he lacked the courage to tell Maria to her face. Caspar's strict order was the impetus he needed.

Still... I don't want to have this conversation...

He had kept putting his unpleasant task aside, and this was the result. While he knew it was his own fault, he couldn't keep from sighing. Nevertheless, he could not back down now.

Angel paused for a moment and looked himself over. Instead of his normal work clothes, he was wearing a Garrison soldier's uniform. He could have waited until after her shift but was afraid his nerves might fade. Thus, he'd brought out the uniform, even though his disguise was already known to the corps and may not serve its purpose.

"Now or never..."

Angel scratched his head, made up his mind, and ploddingly climbed the stairs that led to the watchtower. He passed a number of soldiers on his way, but none of them so much as asked him to stop. Either they didn't notice or were pretending not to, but whichever the case, Angel was thankful.

He could now see the watchtower above. As Angel approached, a soldier stationed within exited sluggishly, perhaps mistaking the craftsman for relief. Raising his hand, Angel nonchalantly stepped inside in his stead.

Maria was there, looking past the Walls with a pair of binoculars. He could see signs of fatigue on her face, but she was the picture of dignity as she stood on duty. She seemed, at first glance, to have gotten over Solm's death, but that was doubtful. No doubt she'd donned the uniform as support, both mentally and physically, consciously placing a lid on her emotions.

Just as Angel tried to think of a way to begin, she spoke. "That day... I was up here when you went on the expedition, waiting for all of you to return." She was still looking beyond the Walls through her binoculars. "I remember having an awful feeling when the Black Star went up."

"I see."

Angel walked to Maria's side and looked out with her. Scanning the area, he saw no Titans. But that was only what he could see. He knew there were Titans lurking here and there.

"It was just a week ago that I was down there…"

Angel had ventured beyond the Wall because he hadn't known just how fearsome it was out there. The Titans were absurdly strong, and the world ridiculously broad. The more you learned, the more you understood how miniscule you were. It was difficult to leave the Walls unless you truly had guts.

But I need to go out there again.

He would develop new gear and use it to overturn the established theory that the Titans didn't die. It was his mission now. He knew it was reckless, and if he could have helped it, he wouldn't go out there. But he had to make another expedition happen. Proving that a Titan had died was something he had to do, both for his best friend and for the life to be born.

This won't get us anywhere, though…

Angel hadn't climbed the Wall to become aware of his own mission.

He looked at Maria out of the corner of his eyes, mentally prepared himself, and began, "I'm sorry, Maria. If only I were—"

"Was he impressive?" Maria interrupted, turning her eyes from the world beyond, towards Angel.

"If it wasn't for him, I might not be here today."

"A proud end it must have been."

"I still can't believe that idiot. Sacrificing himself so that everyone else could get away…" Angel had survived as a result, but it didn't do that his savior had succumbed to death himself.

"I'd always thought this day would come."

The specter of death closely followed any soldier enlisted in the Survey Corps.

He could die one day—any soldier's family members and friends felt the same. At the same time, they were prone to nurture a groundless belief: "Well, not him." No matter how irrational, they had to think that in order to stay calm.

"What're you going to do now?"

"I haven't thought about it yet…"

"Will you stay in the Garrison?"

The main reason Maria had done so was to guard the place that Solm returned to. Now that she had lost him, there was no reason for her to stay.

"What about you?"

"I'm going to craft arms to kill the Titans."

"Even though Solm's gone?"

"It's not just about him at this point."

"I think I'm the same way."

"What do you mean?"

"Solm was why I started, but I'm proud of this job now."

"So you can't quit so readily." That much was evident from how Maria approached her work. "It was a dumb question."

"Yeah, maybe." Maria put on a faint smile. "Of course, I don't think I'll be able to do this for that long."

"Why not?" Angel asked, but he remembered right away. "Well, I hope the baby will be nice and strong."

"Like Solm?"

"I guess we don't know if it'll be a boy."

"Healthy will do for me."

"Too healthy, and we might end up with another Survey Corpsman on our hands."

"I'll worry about that when it happens. I don't think I'd be against it."

"I'm surprised to hear that."

"We're going to be able to defeat the Titans by then, right?" Maria stared Angel in his face with a serious expression. "In that case, I wouldn't be afraid of expeditions. I wouldn't have to wait in fear."

The common sense that Titans could not be killed would be a thing of the past once Angel completed his anti-Titan gear and went on an expedition. And that day would be coming soon.

The kid will be mighty proud of his dad.

While Solm never had the chance to embrace his child, he'd done his duty as a father before passing away.

"Man. What a guy," Angel sighed, turning his gaze past the Walls once more. "I need to put my life to good use, too."

He did not doubt for a moment that it was the only way he could ever repay Solm.

***

"I don't have the materials!" Xenophon sprang into Angel's development lab with a nonsensical outburst. His agitation was manifest from his breathing like a wild horse and his sickly-pale face, but it hardly suited what he'd said.

Having your room invaded as though by some raider just because he didn't "have the materials" was past annoying. Especially if you'd been focused on your work.

"If you're short on materials, just go order some!" Angel shot back, looked away from Xenophon, and turned his concentration back to his hands.

The disassembled parts of the Equipment sat on his work bench. They were sorted into three main groups: the controller, the gas cylinder that held the fuel, and the main unit that connected the two. Each of them had their own problems, both big and small. The big problems were the strength of the wire and the cylinder. These two issues needed to be overcome for the Equipment to be practical. In other words, he had absolutely no spare time to waste on Xenophon.

"They've shut down the distribution channel. I can't even place orders."

"What?" Angel furrowed his brow. "Was the factory city attacked or something?"

"No. Seems like orders from above."

"The old man?"

"Please."

"So then…"

"The royal government."

Xenophon's answer caused Angel's eyes to open wide. "Why are the authorities getting involved in our business?"

"I'd say the talk of shrinking the military is starting to feel real."

"Are the conservatives ramming that through?"

"It's possible."

The conservatives' goal was to shut everyone within the Walls. What kept it from fruition was the fact that they were evenly matched with the reformers, but the shut-ins were gaining force after the Titan invasion.

"If distribution stops, both production and development becomes impossible," Angel said.

"Supplies to the corps will be cut off, too." The first to be affected would be the Survey Corps. "Pretty soon, expeditions will be out of the question."

"Worst case, we're talking about dissolution."

If the Survey Corps were disbanded, there would no cause to go beyond the Walls. There would be no drawbacks to sealing the gates. That had to be the conservatives' roadmap.

"What's the old man doing?"

"He left for a meeting. Sounds like he'll be discussing the matter with workshop chiefs from other towns."

"All right," Angel nodded and set to thinking about how to overcome the situation. He quit before long, however, and turned to face the Equipment that sat before him.

My job is to complete this thing.

Doing so should improve their situation, too.

"Either way, my job is to keep working on this Equipment. That's all I can do."

"It's the same for me, but our supply of materials has been cut off." That was why Xenophon had jumped into the room in a panic.

"So we've played right into their hand…" Angel laughed bitterly, but he couldn't give up. "We're development and production professionals. 'We didn't have the materials' won't cut it."

"Do you have a plan in mind?"

"There are materials lying all over this workshop, aren't there?"

Huge piles of neglected junk had accumulated all around the lab. Though useless in their current form, they could be dismantled and processed to be reborn as workable material. As far as trinkets tantamount to trash went, the workshop was a rich hunting ground, and if necessary, arms awaiting shipment could be reverted back to their materials. For the time being, and for development purposes, they would be fine.

"Okay, let's get started."

Angel reached for a prototype of unclear function that sat on the floor.

***

He'd resumed development on the Equipment because he realized that it could help defeat the Titans. Originally designed to close the gap in height between humans and Titans, the device seemed to be headed in the right direction.

While he once pondered how beneficial investigating the Titans sooner could have been, without all the conditions in place the enemy would have been unassailable. Those conditions had been met now, via locating their weak point and the development of powerful arms. Essential to developing those arms, however, was the discovery of new materials, namely Iron Bamboo and Iceburst Stone. Furthermore, if not for the factory city, those materials would have remained beyond their capacity to process. It was thanks to all the gears miraculously meshing that preparations were finally in place for a counterattack.

The Titans' weakness was their throat. This was Angel's guess based on where Solm blew himself up. While still unconfirmed, he was sure that whatever organ corresponded to the human heart resided there.

But they were up against ridiculous monsters who revived themselves without ado even after having their skulls split. Underestimating them spelled death.

"The short sword can cut their throats open… The question is that Equipment," Xenophon, staring at it, groaned as if in the grips of a fever.

Although they'd happily secured materials by collecting junk from around the workshop, they lacked so much as a clue on how to solve the Equipment's durability issue. As a result, ruptured cylinders piled up in the development lab in what looked like a mountain of returned stock. Still they pushed on, continuing to make one test model after the next, and eventually succeeded in creating a reasonably strong cylinder.

But it's only reasonably strong…

Anything they made would be meaningless unless it was polished enough to entrust one's life to.

"We're going to have to use Iron Bamboo, after all."

"That's the only way to get the toughness we need," Xenophon seconded.

Though they were agreed on using Iron Bamboo, with distribution halted by the royal government it would be extremely hard to get any. They had some scraps left from manufacturing the short swords and the capture net, but not enough for trial and error.

"Should we collect some without permission? We do know where it is."

"Theft should be our last resort. If they catch us, we'll be marked as traitors and they'll chop our heads off," Angel said, waving a leveled hand across his throat.

"I would greatly prefer to be remembered as the savior of humanity. I'd rather not sully my name."

"Remembered or not, we need to leave results."

Angel grabbed a node of Iron Bamboo and began toying with it. Their inventory consisted of a few pieces cut into nodes, and there was little they could do with that amount.

"We managed to do something about the wire…"

Like the cylinder, the wire had toughness problems, but this was fixed by using the web from the Titan capture net. While it hadn't sufficed to keep down a Titan, the wire was certainly strong enough to support a human. There was no substitute for a gas cylinder, though, so they had no choice but to make one.

"I just wish we had a little more of this stuff," regretted Xenophon.

"Do we turn the Iron Bamboo in the short swords back into raw materials?"

"Unfortunately, the only short sword here is the one prototype I made."

"I don't suppose we could recall the rest from the Survey Corps."

"They're the ones who'll be doing the fighting. Can't fight a Titan if you don't have weapons."

"Yeah…" The Equipment and weapons worked as a set. One was meaningless without the other.

"What about reducing the Iron Bamboo content? We'll lose some durability, but it'll still be better than what we have."

"That's one way."

"You don't look like you agree."

"Nope," Angel flatly admitted.

Xenophon's proposal would better a difficult situation. No one would find fault if they adopted it.

But it's not the best solution.

As a craftsman, it was only natural for that to be Angel's goal.

"So, what to do." Angel stared at the Iron Bamboo in his hand, waiting for an idea to hit him. He knew, though, that inspiration didn't descend as if from heaven. The answers all lay within himself.

He resentfully glared at the Iron Bamboo.

The bamboo, a muted silver, was a top ingredient, provided by nature, and there was no greater joy for a craftsman than to work with it. If only they could use Iron Bamboo, he had the confidence to create the ultimate gas cylinder.

Do we steal more knowing the risks, or do we make do with what we have?

Neither choice appealed to Angel, but at this rate development would only be delayed further. He couldn't obsess over materials and end up having the Equipment shelved.

"Processing, huh?" Angel muttered as he flicked the stem with his finger. Lending his ear to the high-pitched sound, he felt something nag at him.

"Let's try going to the Trost District workshop. There might be some Iron Bamboo left there."

"Iron Bamboo…"

"They distributed some to workshops in every town. We could probably find some if we looked around."

"Bamboo…"

"Is something wrong?"

"No, I just like the sound it makes."

"This is no time to be taking it easy." Xenophon shrugged in disbelief. "As you know, bamboo is hollow. That makes the sound resonate."

"Hollow…"

Just as Angel repeated after Xenophon, he understood. Not that bamboo was hollow, but what was nagging at him.

"We've been doing this wrong."

"Excuse me?"

"Our instincts as craftsmen must have gotten in the way."

"What are you trying to say?"

"When we were given the Iron Bamboo, we saw it as a material to be processed."

"Of course we did."

"Because we're craftsmen," Angel agreed with a nod. "But what if we don't need to process it?"

"Pardon me?"

"I'm saying that we've had our cylinders here all along," Angel said with a grin, passing the Iron Bamboo to Xenophon. "This is our cylinder."

"Oh, I see! What an idea!!" Xenophon grasped Angel's intent with due speed. "So we use its properties as bamboo."

"Bamboo is hollow. All we need to do is put gas inside and we have our cylinder."

"And it's Iron Bamboo, so no durability problems."

"Exactly," Angel replied, brimming with confidence.

He felt he was on to something. They had solved their biggest problem, durability. Now they just had to knuckle down and start manufacturing the Equipment. It wouldn't be long until they were done.

"All right, let's get started."

***

Development of the Equipment moved forward surprisingly smoothly, coming together in just a few days.

It had required neither sleepless nights nor miracles, as the real work only consisted of swapping the Equipment's wire and cylinder. While they thought that it would be a long process at first, that was not the case once they discovered the solutions to their problems. It seemed like a joke: to make the wire, they simply unbound Angel's capture net and respun the material, and for the cylinder, what they had on hand served whole.

As the cylinder had shrunk in size, they also made a few minor changes to the Equipment. Now smaller and lighter, the energy source was relocated from the back to the sides of the hips, and they now used two controllers instead of one. While the system was designed to keep working even if one of the controllers was damaged, using both together would allow a user to even climb over Wall Maria. As they could not obtain Iceburst Stone, they filled the cylinders with natural gas, but the Equipment still functioned well. Fuel efficiency was poor, however, making it unsuitable for long periods of use. In order to properly implement the Equipment, they needed Iceburst Stone. All they had to do to fix that was to prove the Titans could be killed.

Still, wait as they might, no reply came from Jorge. The rumors that Wall Maria would be sealed were growing louder by the day, and, as if to lend credence, the royal government started to merge and close down workshops. Angel's was no exception, and regular operations were temporarily halted. While he and Xenophon ignored this and continued working, they could feel the situation worsening by the moment.

Angel and those around him were the only ones who saw it as a crisis, though. The residents seemed to pay no mind. They knew nothing about the world outside the Walls, and their daily lives bore no relation to it. The gates shutting wouldn't have any impact on them. For the residents of Shiganshina District in particular, such a decision was in fact welcome. Angel recognized it as a major crossroads affecting humanity's future, but only a small minority saw things his way. The vast majority of residents had no room in their lives to imagine what the future held. What mattered to them was their livelihoods here and now.

Angel patiently awaited Jorge's reply, but the situation was only getting worse. Public opinion supported sealing the gates, and Angel knew that it was only a matter of time before that became a reality. He didn't know how much emphasis the conservatives placed on the issue, but sealing the gates would be the best way for them to choke the life out of the reformers. They would be pursuing their objective aggressively. The only way to stop them was to take down a Titan during an expedition.

No longer able to sit still, Angel grabbed the Equipment and headed to the Survey Corps barracks together with Xenophon. It was of course to make a direct appeal to Jorge about going on another expedition.

They had nothing to lose. It would be a cruel joke if the Equipment had to be shelved, never to see the light of day. Though Angel was prepared to be turned away, he was shocked at how easily he was granted an audience.

***

"Things are really starting to look ugly."

The mood in the barracks was heavy, and every soldier wore a dark expression as though misfortune had come to someone they knew. It was easy to guess that their situation was similar to the craftsmen's.

A soldier led Angel and Xenophon to the commander's executive chamber.

It was hard to imagine the Survey Corps doing administrative work, but it seemed as though once you reached as high a rank as commander, you had to fight both on and off the battlefield. The small office, no larger than ten square meters, was mostly occupied by a broad desk. On it were piles of documents stacked high.

Instead of a sword, Jorge, the room's master, held a pen in his hands as he silently worked through the documents. Either tired of office work, or distressed over the Survey Corps' future—possibly both—he looked exhausted.

"You look busy," Angel noted.

"I'm not cut out for administrative work. I think I'd be much better off punishing my body," Jorge replied with a stern face. "You're here to talk about an expedition, right?"

"That was fast. Did you harangue him to death?"

"Like I could," Angel brushed off Xenophon's question. "I've only requested it once after the last expedition. That makes this the second time," he continued, and stepped forward. "I want you to give me an answer."

"As you may have already guessed, I cannot grant your request. That's my answer," Jorge told him in a flat, colorless voice.

As Jorge pointed out, Angel had been prepared to be denied. Still, the reality of losing his last glimmer of hope stung him. "I suppose you'd already have contacted me if you wanted to go on an expedition…"

"I do want to."

"What?!" Angel's voice cracked.

"You must be facing some rather annoying circumstances," surmised Xenophon.

"Orders from above, huh?"

"Simply put, yes," Jorge replied gravely and balled his hand into a fist. It was clear what that signified. Of everyone affected by the Survey Corps being unable to go on an expedition, Jorge was the most frustrated of all.

"An indefinite freeze on expeditions. Directive on status of Survey Corps to follow. That's our current situation."

"So you'd like to go, but can't." Xenophon looked persuaded, but Angel was not.

The Survey Corps would soon be dissolved if nothing was done. Once that happened, it would be too late to do anything.

Angel closed in on Jorge. "Are you telling me that the commander of the Survey Corps is just meekly backing down?"

"H-Hey. Don't you think you're being a little rude?"

Xenophon was visibly uncomfortable, but Angel was shielded by his sense of duty, standing tall despite the presence Jorge exuded. Escaping a near-death situation outside the Walls must have toughened his nerves, too. There was nothing in the world more outrageous than the Titans, so nothing could frighten Angel any longer.

"The only way to change the situation is to produce results. And that's possible now." Angel placed the Equipment on the desk. "This is the machine we use to kill a Titan."

"A Titan? With this?" Jorge looked at the Equipment with a baffled expression as though he had seen a ghost. To Jorge, who didn't know how to use the Equipment, it must have looked like a mysterious contraption.

"Solm showed us that the Titans can be killed. You saw it, didn't you?"

"If you can call what happened to that Titan death, yes."

"It would be a different story if the corpse stayed on the field," remarked Xenophon. Indeed the situation would be quite different had the Titan's corpse not disappeared. Still, in terms of eliminating a threat, the outcome equaled death.

"In order to keep the Survey Corps from being dissolved, we need to show everyone that the Titans can be killed."

"Are you telling me to ignore orders from above?"

If a commander flaunted rules and regulations, he would be setting a bad example for his subordinates. It would surely lower morale, too. The conservative leaders would seize the opportunity and move to dissolve the Survey Corps.

"Your plan could threaten the existence of the Survey Corps."

"I can see that…"

"And you want me to accept it?"

Jorge glared at Angel as if to intimidate him, but the pressure was not enough to make him waver.

Jorge isn't what I'm afraid of.

What Angel feared was his own heart buckling to his terror of the Titans.

He met Jorge's stare. "Only if you want to sway destiny."

"Don't you think you're asking for a little much?" Xenophon timidly interceded.

Angel was fully aware that he was. Yet, he could not back down.

"Do you really think you're worth betting the future of the Survey Corps on?"

"I say you're not looking at it the right way."

"What do you mean?

"What Solm entrusted us with isn't the future of the Survey Corps. It's something bigger, no?"

"True. What needs protecting isn't the organization called the Survey Corps."

"So you'll go?"

Though Angel's face was already beaming, Jorge shook his head sideways. "It's the soldiers' lives that'll be on the line, not yours. It'll be their responsibility, too. And mine, of course."

"You're saying my proposal is mere talk?"

"I'm just stating the facts."

Angel had not planned to leave everything up to the Survey Corps, however. "I'll come with you."

"You? You're joking, right?!" Jorge seemed to honestly wonder this and could not help but show it. "After that terrible ordeal, you say you're able to step into the jaws of death?"

"Unless I go, how—"

"Well, I do know. Once you've seen as many soldiers crumble as I have, you know," Jorge said before Angel could finish. "Even troops whose minds and bodies have been hardened lose it more or less when they see a Titan. They're monsters, and you know that. A sense of powerlessness plunges many a soul into despair."

"And I'm one of them?"

"At best you'll stand there paralyzed in a pinch. You'll exacerbate our losses."

Jorge's point, which seemed to allude to Solm's death, gave Angel pause.

"Why don't we leave it at that?" Xenophon cut into their exchange. "Any more and you'll just be jerking open your wound."

Angel appreciated Xenophon's consideration, but he couldn't give up even if it meant blood pouring out of the crack in his heart.

"If you people won't go, then I'm going alone."

"You know that's impossible!" Xenophon objected.

"I'm serious."

"I see how strong your resolve is, but we can't let a civilian past the Walls," Jorge replied to Angel after a moment of mute deliberation. "But that doesn't settle it for you, does it. So I'll give you a chance."

"A chance?"

"If you can beat me in a fight, do as you wish."

"And if I lose?"

"You give up."

"Okay. Simple, I like it."

Angel nodded to Jorge.

An agitated outburst came from Xenophon.

"Give it a little more thought! He's a pro. You have no chance of winning. It's absolutely hopeless!"

"It's only an overwhelming disadvantage. There is hope."

"You know, there's such a thing as being too optimistic…"

"I have *this*."

Whether the Equipment was effective against humans was still a cipher.

Since Jorge didn't know its abilities, Angel could at least count on surprising him with it. Even a battle-hardened veteran who marshaled the Survey Corps would show some sort of opening. If Angel had any chance of winning, it was with that.

"Sorry, Angel?" Xenophon whispered. "He never said you could use

that thing."

"Ah…" Angel let out a small, yelping scream and fearfully looked Jorge's way.

"Let's change locations," Jorge told Angel as he stood up from his chair.

He already seemed to be prepared to fight, and his expression was stern enough to make a wild beast flinch. Being freed from the bonds of paperwork seemed to usher back his ferocity.

"I'll handle your funeral preparations at least," Xenophon promised unhelpfully.

***

It seemed as though an announcement had been made that the commander would be putting a cocky civilian in his place. A crowd of a few dozen had spontaneously formed in front of the barracks. Ninety percent of them were Survey Corps soldiers, while the rest were traders and merchants who conducted business with the corps. They all gazed upon Jorge with intense anticipation, not a single one of them paying any attention to Angel.

"I don't like this."

Angel felt like a soldier stranded in enemy territory. He could tell by the mood that the crowd essentially viewed him in that way, too.

"You brought this situation upon yourself. Don't forget that," reminded Xenophon.

"What a pal you are. But you'll avenge me if I lose, right?"

"Please. I'd prefer to stay alive for the time being," the older craftsman promptly declined.

"I'll give you a small advantage," Jorge offered, his face brimming with confidence. "You can use that Equipment of yours. I'd like to see how it works, too." He added, "I'll fight you unarmed. You win if you can land a single attack on me."

"Confident, aren't you?"

"Well, I'm not new to the combat arts."

"Don't get worked up and pull that sword from your hip."

Jorge stood there calmly as if to invite Angel to come at him from any angle. Carelessly jumping in would no doubt elicit a merciless counter-punch.

"What a lucky break. A one-in-a-thousand chance. You might even pull off that impossible upset."

In other words, according to Xenophon he still had a near-zero chance of winning.

"This is turning into one hell of a product unveiling…"

Angel gauged the Equipment on his body and breathed out.

So the first combat it sees is against a human, huh.

The human in question, moreover, was the commander of the Survey Corps. An able adversary, all too able.

There's basically no chance of me winning.

That's what an impossible upset meant. But he didn't have to beat Jorge.

If I can make him slip up and get just one shot in…

As modest a miracle as that might be in his powers to occasion.

"Ready?"

His body filling with vigor, Jorge assumed a fighting stance. Angel could sense the ease the man felt as an expert in combat. With an amateur as his opponent, it was only natural for him to appear relaxed.

It's a little late in the game, but this doesn't look good for me.

He couldn't let Jorge take the initiative and dictate the pace of the fight. Angel crouched and retied his shoes. This was in order to dampen Jorge's spirit, but he also grabbed a clump of dirt from the ground.

"All right, let's get this started!" Angel yelled, throwing dirt at Jorge's face at the same time in an attempt to blind him.

Cowardly, aren't I?

But it was no time for Angel to be picky about his tactics. Right now, winning was the most important thing of all.

Angel kicked against the ground, quickly closed the distance between himself and Jorge, and hoisted up his right arm. It was a flashy, obviously amateur move, but with his enemy's sight compromised, he didn't fear a counterattack.

Angel tightly balled up his fist and swung for Jorge's face. With no combat experience, he had no idea how powerful the blow was. But if it hit, it would surely put a dent in Jorge's cool demeanor.

But Jorge stopped Angel's punch as though it were nothing, then twisted his right wrist. Angel's forearm turned, naturally causing him to fall on the ground. From there, his strong arm was pressed to his back in a hammerlock. It all happened in a flash, and the joints in his arm and shoulder cried out in pain at once.

"Good attack. You never know what to expect on the battlefield. Letting your guard down for a single moment could cost you your life."

Jorge released the submission hold. Angel had tried to rattle him and to sneak in an attack, but the plan had failed spectacularly.

He got up and shook his aching arm a few times to check if it still worked. There was still a dull pain in his wrist, elbow, and shoulder joints, but they were still fully functional. If Jorge had applied just a little more pressure, though, Angel would surely either have broken bones or destroyed joints.

"Ahh, your only chance…" Xenophon said, holding his head in his hands.

"My 'only'? Don't say that."

But it was the truth.

If a surprise attack won't work, then I'll just have to go with a straightforward one…

When and how he brought the Equipment into play would be key. Jorge had no idea about its mechanism, so Angel moving vertically had to be unimaginable. Even a man of his level would surely show an opening or two.

I guess I have to rely on surprise attacks all the way.

Angel looked around and found a number of targets for his anchors, such as the barracks and trees.

The question is whether I'll hit them or not.

He had test-fired the Equipment a number of times, but significant training was needed in order to accurately hit a target with the anchors.

You could hit a gigantic target like a wall with your eyes closed, but technique was required to hit a small target such as a tree trunk, especially in the middle of combat.

Hold the controller carefully, as though you were sniping, fix your aim on your target, then pull the lever: you needed to do all of that in order to be accurate, but it meant exposing yourself in a defenseless state. A Titan would probably pay no mind, but not Jorge.

"If you're not going to make a move, then I will," the commander abruptly interrupted his challenger's thoughts.

By the time Angel realized what was going on, Jorge was already in front of him. Although being caught off-guard while planning out a surprise attack was the height of folly, Angel at least managed to guard his face with both hands, an impressive feat for an amateur.

"Guard high and you're open low." Jorge's fist sank into Angel's defenseless solar plexus.

"Nghh…"

Angel's body bent over, and his breathing stopped for a moment. At the same time, he felt such intense pain rush over him that he thought he might black out. Hardly able to stand, he clutched his abdomen and collapsed to his knees. Tears welled in his eyes, and the contents of his stomach rushed back up and spewed out of his mouth. He curled up into a fetal position, cowering atop his own vomit. He was half-conscious, making the pain in his stomach hard to bear; simply passing out would surely have been easier on him. Jorge had no doubt intentionally punched him with the perfect amount of strength to get this result.

Give me a break, brawling isn't my specialty…

Angel tried to curse Jorge but couldn't speak the words aloud.

"Is that all you have for me?" Jorge's disappointed voice rained down on Angel. "Maybe I overestimated you."

Jorge reached out his hand, possibly to deliver the finishing blow.

Damn it… I'm not going to let it end here.

Still crouched, Angel felt around for his holster and pulled his controller's lever. The Equipment groaned, and compressed gas shot out of a nozzle.

167

"Hunh?!" Jorge grunted in a baffled tone and jumped backward, putting some distance between himself and Angel.

Angel hadn't shot an anchor, only releasing a small bit of gas, but it was enough to make Jorge cautious. It seemed like a pathetic last-ditch tactic, but beggars couldn't be choosers, and Angel needed to get back up.

Still, it wasn't easy to shake off the damage Jorge had dealt, and he wouldn't be so kind as to wait for Angel to recover. This was a real fight. At the very least, Jorge was treating it as one. Angel could no longer afford to keep the Equipment's abilities a secret in hopes of a surprise attack.

He aimed the muzzle of the controller at the second floor of the barracks, a relatively simple target to hit. He sunk an anchor in it and quickly pulled his body upward. Flying was out of the question even for Jorge, so Angel could attempt to recover from the damage he'd taken. It was a cowardly tactic, but the Equipment was the only advantage he had. He'd do anything to win.

"I see. An interesting device."

Jorge had taken an honest interest in the Equipment, as did the soldiers looking on. Their reaction was natural: while it didn't allow Angel to fly, they'd seen him move in an unthinkable way that ignored gravity. They had probably realized the potential of the Equipment, too, and were sure to come up with tactics Angel couldn't even imagine, employing them on the field. Angel's chest filled with excitement, as this was the best possible unveiling ceremony, but it would all be meaningless if they could never use the Equipment against a Titan.

He rubbed his aching stomach and calmed his breathing.

I should have had Solm spar with me…

As he laughed bitterly, the pain in his stomach subsided a bit. He loosened the wire and returned to the ground, then yanked the anchor still stuck to the wall and sent it back into the muzzle.

"You can aim at the Titans' weak point if you have this."

"But how will it do against me?"

Jorge taunted Angel with a beckoning gesture, but Angel's knees were still weak from the earlier attack, leaving him in no shape to approach Jorge.

But I do have a way of getting around.

Angel held the controller horizontally, aiming its muzzle toward Jorge. The man stood about five meters away, but it was a tree trunk behind him that Angel was targeting.

Seven or eight meters away. Please hit…

Praying, he lightly fixed his aim and pulled the lever to shoot out an anchor.

Jorge seemed to think that Angel was aiming at him. He drew his short sword with a backhanded grip and used its pommel to deflect the oncoming anchor. It veered off course and landed far from its target.

"Just as I'd expect from the commander of the Survey Corps. Such incredible kinetic vision and reflexes," Xenophon marveled, clapping, but Angel was in no place to join along.

He had no time to recover his anchor and aim again. He tossed the controller aside, then pulled the lever on his other controller. The anchor slipped past Jorge and dug into the tree trunk. Angel's body took to the air.

No tricks! I'll charge straight into him!

The moment he manipulated the lever, Angel flew toward Jorge head-first like a bullet.

Jorge immediately dropped into a fighting stance and pulled his right elbow back slightly. He began to deliver a short, close-quarters blow with his muscular arm.

For a moment, Angel's eyes met with Jorge's.

Did he just smile?

Before he could check again, a sensation like a hammer smashing into his face shot through him. He felt himself fading rapidly, and his vision began to grow dark.

Did I do it?

But before he could make certain, Angel blacked out.

***

A jolt of pain shot through Angel, who'd been sleeping like a log. It was so intense that it nearly made him jump, but his body was unresponsive, and he couldn't even scream. His body burned feverishly and ached from head to toe. His face hurt most of all, and it was so swollen that his eyes could not open past a squint. It was obvious to him that he was hurt, but he could not understand why he was in such a predicament.

"Where am I..."

Angel pulled his eyelids up with his fingers in an attempt to glean any information he could from whatever vision he was able to muster.

"The development lab?"

Repeated experiments and small fires had left the ceiling of the room dirty and covered in soot. In other words, Angel was back in his headquarters, and as he scanned his surroundings, just moving his eyes, he discerned a room filled with a jumble of items. He was lying on the bed of his development room.

"What happened again?"

He could tell by the light coming through the window that it was around noon. It felt as though he had been sleeping for a while, as his stomach began to grumble as soon as he woke. Aside from his injuries, his body seemed to be functioning fine.

Angel gathered his strength and will and used his arms to raise his torso out of bed. His body ached horribly, but he was able to move as long as he could block out the pain.

From Angel's face, contorted in agony, fell a warm, wet washcloth. He placed it against his throbbing cheek and looked down at his body to find discolored, reddish-black bloodstains splattered on his work clothes.

So... What happened to me?

As he began to think again, the door to his development lab slowly started to open.

"Finally awake?"

Maria entered the room with an appalled expression.

"How long was I sleeping?"

"Around a full day."

Maria let out a deep sigh as she walked toward Angel. "I knew you were an idiot, but I didn't think you were this much of a moron."

"What do you mean?"

"You sparred with the commander, didn't you?"

"Oh, right. I fought Jorge and—"

He couldn't remember what had happened after that but could guess the outcome from his outstretched position on the bed. The swelling and pain in his face backed up his conclusion.

While it hurt him to do so, it seemed as though he had no choice but to admit defeat.

He was just too strong for me.

Angel was proud of himself for having the courage to challenge the commander of the Survey Corps, but it was all meaningless if he couldn't win.

I wish I'd at least got a shot in on him.

That Angel couldn't was proof of Jorge's extraordinary abilities.

"Too bad. They probably could have put the Equipment to good use."

"But you won, didn't you? Your efforts paid off."

"I won? I did?!"

"Xenophon was saying that the commander lost by disqualification."

"Disqualification…"

Angel searched through his memories but couldn't think of Jorge doing anything unfair. The man wasn't the type to cheat, and all Angel could recall was a pro graciously giving a lesser opponent a lesson.

"He said Jorge drew his short sword."

Angel suddenly remembered and understood. "He's admitting defeat just because of that?"

"I think it means that winning and losing didn't matter to him."

"Didn't matter?"

"It means he saw your resolve."

"So that's why he wanted to fight? That's a pretty rough way of doing it," Angel snorted, frowning sourly.

"It's the kind of thing he'd do."

If Angel had lacked conviction, the blow to his abdomen alone might have incapacitated him.

"I think the commander is dying to go on an expedition, too. He just couldn't agree to it because of his position."

"And he'd definitely face punishment if he disobeyed an order."

Jorge was responsible for his subordinates and their families, which had to weigh heavily on his shoulders. So much responsibility surely turned decision-making into an ordeal. Angel had no baggage in that regard.

"He says the expedition is in a week."

"The expedition?! So Jorge—"

"He must have made up his mind."

In other words, Jorge was embarking on an expedition fully prepared to resign from his post as commander.

"The Survey Corps and a few others concerned are the only ones who know. If disciplinary measures are all we end up facing, we'll consider ourselves fortunate."

"So you're in."

"I'll be the one opening the gate that day."

"What about your colleagues?" Angel asked.

"There's no way I could tell them," Maria said, shaking her head no. "There are a lot of people with conservative streaks in the Garrison. If they found out about the expedition, there's a real chance of a leak."

"Are you really okay with this?"

"Yeah. I've already made up my mind."

Whatever the outcome of the expedition, everyone would surely be punished. Common soldiers would be dishonorably discharged and forced into a life of shame. Veteran's benefits they were slated to receive would be revoked, too. Guided though they might be by their convictions, it was all too risky an act.

Maria seemed prepared, though, and her bright expression was free of doubts.

"We've already come this far. I'm sure it'll go well."

"Yeah."

Angel did feel anxious. It wasn't as if he'd cleansed himself of his fear of the Titans. Yet, he was confident that the expedition would be a success.

All the conditions have been met. All that's left is to take down a Titan.

There was something he had to do first, though.

"Couldn't he have gone a little easier on me?"

Angel rubbed his swollen face.

***

Roughly thirty people would participate in the expedition. It would consist of the entire Survey Corps, led by Jorge, and Angel. As they would be disobeying orders, participation was voluntary, but every Survey Corps soldier was determined to go. That, however, was only natural. One did not sign up for the Survey Corps, a group never far from death, without being at least somewhat of an oddball. Part of the mystery that was the Titans stood to be revealed, and missing the chance to witness the historic moment was unthinkable. That alone was enough motivation for them to go on the expedition, and the Equipment's potential also stirred them.

They would only have one unit of the essential tool. It should have been supplied to every soldier, but couldn't be manufactured with no Iron Bamboo available. The silver lining was that they'd already distributed the short swords.

It was decided that Angel would represent the group and wear the Equipment. Someone outside of the Survey Corps participating in an expedition was rare enough, let alone his partaking in combat, but no one could use the Equipment as well as Angel. Though he could hardly be described as a practiced hand, Jorge had determined that the maneuvers he'd demonstrated during their mock battle sufficed. Still, Angel was an amateur. It went without saying that the Survey Corps would be running a great deal of interference for him.

I guess you could call it fate.

Wearing the Equipment himself and fighting Titans wasn't what he'd envisioned.

But I suppose I'm glad it turned out this way...

He now had the opportunity to kill a Titan with a device he'd developed, so he ought to be happy. That was not all. He'd be able to show off the usefulness of the Equipment and prove that the Titans could be defeated.

And I can avenge Solm and Corina.

In other words, Angel had the chance to settle things personally. There was nothing for him to complain about.

The only question is if I'll be able to handle a Titan.

Titans were not only large but strong and difficult to kill. Their behavior, however, followed incredibly simple principles. In order to defeat Jorge, Angel would have to train in all aspects of combat and spend many hours on the battlefield, but against a Titan, there was no need for mind games. It was more like exterminating a giant pest.

Angel spent the week leading up to the expedition training with the Equipment. He kept flying through the air over and over until it felt like an extension of his own body, until it was as natural as breathing. The process left his body covered in bruises, but he felt able to call himself the foremost expert at wielding the Equipment. Whether this would be of any use on the battlefield, though, was a different question.

Angel stood in front of Wall Maria and glared at the towering barrier. It was difficult to train for a fight against a Titan, but he could visualize the battle by picturing the wall to be his enemy. Angel concentrated and began to form the image of a Titan against the wall.

The Titans' weak point is their throat. I tear it open.

With a practice sword in his right hand and a controller gripped in his left, Angel slowly let out a breath.

All right!

Angel fixed his controller's aim on his image of the Titan. He shot an anchor, and it plunged into the Titan's throat. The moment he verified this, he flew into the air, leapt straight to its weak point, and swiped sideways with his practice sword. Once he completed the smooth chain of maneuvers, his mental image disappeared, leaving behind the familiar face of the wall.

"All that's left is to face a real one…"

Angel had brought down dozens of imaginary Titans, but the one that mattered was the real Titan he would be facing.

"It all comes down to tomorrow."

Angel touched Wall Maria with his hand and turned his thoughts to the outside world.

***

It was when he was relaxing in his development lab that the situation suddenly changed.

Summoned by Caspar, Angel walked to the chief's office. Jorge was waiting for him there with a grim look. The commander's sour face indicated that something serious had happened.

The first thing out of Jorge's mouth was a piece of shocking news: "They've decided to dissolve the Survey Corps."

"Dissolve…" Befuddled, Angel repeated the word, then quickly turned pale as the situation sank in. "What? Why?!"

Angel shot off a barrage of questions, but Jorge merely replied, "Decision from above."

"Then what about the expedition? What's going to happen to the expedition?"

"Back to square one, he says," Caspar relayed the conclusion with a bitter expression.

"The expedition is tomorrow! Canceling it after we've come this far…"

"I feel the same way." Jorge curled his fist. "But I don't have any authority whatsoever at this point."

"Now of all times…"

"One of the royal government's hounds might have worked their way in somewhere."

It seemed possible, but Angel was not interested in tracking down a culprit. What was important was the fate of the expedition.

"After they dissolve the Survey Corps, they'll seal the gates. Once that happens, we'll never be able to ride out again."

It was an illusion in the first place to think that shutting the gates would bring peace. While things would remain placid for a while, it doomed humanity to gently wasting away. As long as they were a walled city, not going past the gates guaranteed a steady decline.

"If we don't do it now, we'll never be able to recover."

"I know."

"If we could just get results, the Survey Corps should be able to avoid dissolution."

"I know that."

"Then…"

Angel wouldn't let go, but Jorge sank into a pensive silence. It was clear that the commander hadn't come to terms with the royal government's decision, but he still seemed hesitant to act, bound by his duty as a corps leader.

Angel could understand Jorge's anguish but didn't have the time to wait for the man to make up his mind. If the decision had been made to dissolve the Survey Corps, the gate could be sealed at any moment.

"Damn it!" Angel spat, turning his back to Jorge and Caspar.

"What're you going to do?" inquired Caspar.

"I'm going to prepare for the expedition."

"Y'know full well that ya can't do it alone."

"I don't care whether I can or not. I'm going," Angel declared and left the chief's office.

***

Cutting a figure was all well and good, but as Caspar pointed out, there could be no expedition if Angel was the only one going. At the very least, he would need one other person to work with him. The only one he could ask to be that person was Maria, a Garrison soldier and protector of the Walls.

Angel walked to the barracks.

The three-story facility provided housing for the majority of the soldiers stationed in Shiganshina District, including Maria.

"So you want me to just watch as you go off to get yourself killed?" Maria expressed her disagreement in no uncertain terms after Angel explained the circumstances. "How could I help you if the Survey Corps won't be going with you?"

"Now is our only chance. We're going to regret it if we don't take it." Using the Equipment to defeat a Titan and avenge his fallen comrades—he wasn't letting such an incredible opportunity slip away before his eyes.

"Why don't you wait until the commander has a change of heart?"

Angel would have considered Maria's plan had he had time. Jorge was sure to eventually collect his thoughts and opt in favor of an expedition. But they could not afford a single moment of delay. They had to make up their minds immediately and save any regrets for later. If the gates were shut, they would have no course of action.

"If they do seal the gates, it's not like they'd do it today or tomorrow, right? I haven't heard of any orders like that, either."

"The dissolution of the Survey Corps was sudden, too. Anything could happen."

"But…"

Maria remained opposed to Angel's plan. She had probably already arrived at a conclusion, and it was the same for Angel. In short, they could keep arguing and never see eye to eye.

"Okay, fine." Angel said, half-forcefully bringing the conversation to a stop.

"I think waiting a little is the right thing to do." Maria breathed a sigh of relief, believing she had dissuaded Angel.

"I'm going on an expedition tomorrow morning, as planned."

"What?" Maria opened her eyes wide. "But if I'm not there, the gates…"

"I can go outside without your help."

Scaling Wall Maria would be simple if he used the Equipment to lift himself over it. If there was a problem, it was that he would not have a mount.

"I guess I don't have a choice, then." Maria let out a deep sigh. "I just need to open the gates like you asked, right?"

"You're okay with it?"

"Of course I'm not!" Maria immediately snapped back. "But if you're going to go even if I tell you not to, I don't have a choice."

"I see. I'm sorry."

"Like you mean it," Maria shrugged.

"Okay. I'll be counting on you tomorrow, then. Just like we planned."

"Please don't do anything too stupid."

"I know."

"Promise?"

"Promise."

"Liar," Maria accused before holding Angel tight. "I don't care if you kill a Titan or not. Just promise me you'll come back alive."

These were surely Maria's honest thoughts. Her hatred of the Titans was outweighed by her desire to not lose anyone else. Angel felt the same way, too.

"I promise," Angel replied.

***

As the saying goes, it's always darkest before dawn, and it was hard to make out faces and figures in the dim light before the sun rose. It was dark enough to have to ask who you were speaking to, but Angel knew that it was Xenophon by his side as they had left the workshop together.

"All ready?"

"I have the Equipment, and I have one of your short swords. I have a whole bunch of explosives ready, too. I'm good to go," Angel said coolly as he mounted his horse.

"You don't seem nervous."

"I am. How could I not be scared?"

He would be exiting the gates alone to go defeat a Titan. Normally his body would be shaking and his mind completely blank. Nevertheless, the situation was so unreal that his senses had been numbed, and thankfully his body was no more tense than it needed to be.

"Part of me wants to go with you, but sadly, I don't have the courage. I apologize."

"It takes courage to admit your weaknesses, doesn't it?"

"I'm happy you said that," Xenophon admitted.

It did not seem right to call a solo expedition an act of courage, though. Angel recognized that he was confusing recklessness with bravery, but he still believed that things would somehow work out. He'd have a difficult time answering why, but all the conditions for killing a Titan had been met. Perhaps the answer was that he didn't see why he *couldn't* kill a Titan.

"I don't need to say farewell, do I?"

"Of course not. I'll be right back."

"Then may fortune be with you."

Angel nodded and started to ease his horse forward. The town and its people were in a deep slumber, and not a soul stood on the avenue leading to the gate. It was eerily silent, the only sounds around him his horse's steps and its breathing. The town would wake in another hour and return the avenue to its usual hustle and bustle.

That, or there's going to be a huge uproar.

If the main gate was opened with seemingly no notice or reason, the residents were sure to be disturbed. They would be reminded of the day that a Titan barged into their town. Of course, the gates would only be open for half a minute, and it was still early morning. The number of witnesses would likely be few.

Angel gradually approached the Wall. According to the plan, Maria would be waiting in the watchtower above, ready to open the gates.

He suddenly started to feel nervous, but unlike on the previous expedition, he remained calm. He had made meticulous plans, eliminating uncertain factors as much as possible so that dealing with a Titan would be like routine paperwork. True, it was an incredibly difficult mission, ridiculous, reckless, and rash, but it certainly was not an impossible one.

"Time to say goodbye to my nightmares, too."

Angel grabbed a flare gun, pointed the muzzle above his head, and pulled the trigger. A White Star exploded in the sky, filling everything around him with a bright light as if to herald dawn.

"Daybreak comes a little earlier today."

He looked away from the White Star overhead and directed his eyes straight in front of him.

At that very moment, a single cavalry suddenly appeared—or rather, he had been there from the start, only unseen in the darkness.

"True to your words, I see."

"Are you here to stop me?"

Angel sat up defensively as he gazed at the stately mounted figure. It was Jorge.

"I think you'd be sprawled out on the ground by now if that were the case."

"Then why are you here?"

"Thought I'd offer what little help I could. That's why we're all here."

Angel was confused, but he heard the surging sound of galloping horses behind him.

"The Survey Corps... Are you sure?!"

"It wouldn't be accurate to say that." Jorge pointed to the back of his cloak.

"Your emblem..."

The winged emblem identifying him as a member of the Survey Corps was nowhere to be found on Jorge's cape, with frayed cloth visible there instead. He must have removed it with his own hands.

"What a bunch of damned fools."

Just as Angel moaned out the words, the gates that led beyond the Walls began to roar open. Birds took flight across the city, seemingly frightened by the sound.

"Okay, let's go!"

Angel broke away to take the lead as Jorge and the soldiers followed behind. As the gates loomed closer and closer, Angel looked up as though he had suddenly remembered something. He saw Maria up in the watchtower, bathed in dawn's first rays. He smiled at her divine appearance.

As if to rebuff the group, a dust-filled gust of wind swept in from the desolate plain, but it was hardly enough to make them shrink away. Angel steeled his will and broke off into the hazy, dust-clouded expanse.

***

Angel and the others had set off to accomplish something unheard-of: exterminating a Titan. An hour had passed, though, and they had yet to find their target. It almost seemed as if the Titans had sensed that they were now the hunted and had conferred and fled as one. It was an undeniably deflating situation after they had sortied beyond the Walls in high spirits, but they remained on edge. Anything could happen past the Walls.

The company was on standby about five kilometers south of Shiganshina District. There had been no contact from Team 1, which had gone scouting, but it would surely find a Titan before long.

Just three teams… Their numbers have shrunk a lot.

The Survey Corps had, at one point, as many as eighty members, but now only numbered thirty. They had been split into a precarious arrangement of three teams, led by Jorge and his two deputy commanders. While their organization had always been a small, elite force, there were now too few of them to maintain a Survey Corps.

Angel gazed southward, where Team 1 had disappeared out of sight. The goal may have been to subdue a Titan, but they still wanted to avoid a long sojourn outside. They sat in wait just five kilometers from the town so they could fight a Titan in a more advantageous location. Even if things went wrong, at just five kilometers out, their retreat would be smooth. They could promptly get in firing range of the cannons and have the Titans driven away.

If they'll fire them, of course.

The Garrison had no obligation to save a party that had flaunted the rules and left.

"You've got some guts," Jorge said as he approached Angel. "Why not go ahead and join the Survey Corps?"

"Not funny. This is the last time I do anything this dangerous."

"I think you're surprisingly cut out for it." Jorge sounded like he could be serious, as Angel heard disappointment in his voice.

"They say there's something called the Sea out there," Angel said, pointing south.

"The Sea? What's that?"

"I don't really know, either. I've just heard that over half the world is covered by waters called that."

"Aren't you a know-it-all."

"Solm was."

Jorge looked convinced.

"I don't plan to become a soldier, but I'd love to come back to lay my eyes on the Sea." Angel didn't know if it existed or not, but it was worth seeking out. The story would be the greatest souvenir he could bring to Solm's gravestone. "That's why I need you Survey Corps guys to stand your ground."

"We'll try," Jorge answered solemnly.

Just then, a crimson signal rose in the south sky. It was a Red Star.

"Looks like they found one."

Jorge took out his binoculars and checked the sky to the south.

A few moments later, one Red Star and countless Yellow Stars shot into the air.

"A big one's coming, a ten-plus-meter-class."

Jorge offered his binoculars, and through them Angel glimpsed the hazy figure of a tall, thin young man. The Titan approached quickly, and his fuzzy outline gradually grew sharper. He looked like a heartthrob in his mid-teens. As though upset about something, an irate expression was plastered on his face.

Ahead rose a cloud of dust presumably made by Team 1's horses. Behind it a man-shaped monster charged ahead, bringing with him a rumble in the ground. The Titan was half a kilometer away but still visible to the naked eye. Mammon's size was out of the ordinary, but this Titan rushing toward them like a tsunami was a third larger. Impressive even for a Titan, he was as big as they came.

"Prepare for combat!"

The moment Jorge gave his order, the soldiers took fighting stances, each with a weapon of choice in hand.

There were three hundred meters left between them and the Titan. They had seen many Titans before, but the ten-plus-meter-class monster charging toward them was like a living disaster. The overwhelming presence demanded awe, but human beings possessed the intellect and courage needed to brush such feelings aside and do more than gawk at an incoming threat.

The Titan fiercely rushed toward them, seeking prey. Every step he took rattled the ground and sent vibrations creeping up their feet. When Team 1 rejoined them, the soldiers spread out to intercept the Titan in a V-shaped formation.

"Fire!!"

Carbines exploded simultaneously on Jorge's signal. Bullets dug into the Titan's shoulders, bore holes through his chest, and demolished a part of his head. Yet, his expression unchanged, the Titan neither groaned nor staggered. Scar tissue-like membrane quickly covered the wounds, which began to heal before the soldiers' eyes.

Nevertheless, the Titan stopped after taking a few more steps. As soon as Jorge saw this, he commanded the two wings of the formation to close into a circle that trapped the Titan. A few soldiers moved in with short swords in hand.

"We'll get the Titan's legs. You take his head."

"All right," Angel replied with a stern expression.

Though the Survey Corps would be setting the stage, Angel still had to take on a Titan having had zero experience. It was no surprise that his body was stiffening.

"All your hard work was for this day, was it not? You'll be fine if you just keep your wits about you."

"Yeah… You're right."

Angel took a deep breath and calmed himself, then opened his eyes wide and took in the status of the battle.

The soldiers were weaving back and forth and persistently attacking the Titan's legs. This probably didn't do so much as tickle him, but wounds could still deprive the Titan of his physical capacities, if only for a moment.

"All right!"

Angel gathered his resolve, grabbed his carbine, and pointed it toward the Titan. He used its sights to aim between the Titan's eyebrows, then pulled the trigger. A bullet flew out of the muzzle, causing the gun's barrel to hop backward. Its aim true, the shot buried itself in the Titan's brow, and he jerked his head back as if to take in the sky.

Angel tossed his rifle to the side, gripped a controller in his left hand and his short sword in his right, then pointed the controller's muzzle at the Titan's throat and pulled the lever. The Equipment's main unit groaned at his hip and shot out an anchor. The wind slightly changed its course, and the anchor missed its target and sank into the Titan's chest. It wasn't going as he had visualized, but the result fell within the margin of error.

Solm, Corina…

Angel thought of the two as he summoned up his courage.

"Here goes!"

Angel stepped onto his horse's saddle and jumped into the air. As soon as he did, he set his eyes on the Titan and adjusted the controller's lever.

Gas shot out from the Equipment's nozzle as it began to wind the wire back in. Angel flew toward the Titan's chest like an arrow.

The Equipment momentarily freed its user from the yoke of gravity, but it demanded a high price for the inconceivable movements it enabled. Enough pressure to incapacitate a person bore down on Angel's body, and his face twisted in agony. If he lost even a bit of focus, he courted calamity, but he grit his teeth and withstood the force as he carefully adjusted the lever and lowered his speed to make a soft landing on the Titan's chest.

Angel continued to move, recovering his anchor and grabbing a collarbone to lift himself up. Losing no time, he slashed at the Titan's throat with his short sword. Angel didn't have the strength needed to decapitate the Titan, but the short sword's blade was sharp, digging a wound twenty centimeters deep. It was a more than sufficient blow on a weak point, but there was no such thing as overkill with a Titan. Angel stabbed the Titan's Adam's apple with the sword. Its tip seemed to go far enough to hit bone, as the feeling of something metallically hard traveled through his palm. Whether it was a problem of purity or lax tempering, a faint crack appeared in the blade.

"How's that!"

Angel glared at the Titan. Steam erupted from the wound, engulfing Angel before he could get away.

"Ah!"

The extreme temperature made Angel writhe. It was like being in a sauna, with so much hot air around that it was difficult even to breathe.

He grimaced at the blowing steam and locked eyes with the Titan who'd been facing up.

Angel's eyes grew wide. The Titan's dark black pupils were full of vitality, with no traces of the fleetingness of a dying creature. A strong will dwelled in them. A powerful desire to eat the human Angel.

What's going on?

Before Angel could consider the possibilities, the Titan's hand reached throat-ward.

Angel removed his short sword, then shot an anchor into the Titan's foot, giving himself enough slack to rappel down to the ground.

I felt it. I'm sure I hit his weak point dead-on.

Though he was confused, Angel's mind raced.

If he still won't die, that means…

There was only one conclusion.

Their throat isn't their weak point?

With three meters left, the Titan's arm caught in Angel's wire, causing him to swing widely to the side. The momentum dislodged the anchor, and Angel flew into the air.

Dammit!

Angel cursed in his heart.

He'd reel the anchor back in, then shoot it back into the Titan. Or move to another target—

The sequence of actions ran through the back of Angel's head, but he had neither the time nor the reflexes for it. Perhaps if he'd been holding his other controller instead of his short sword, but it was sitting in its holster.

So you need to use both hands to have meaningful control.

Just as he realized this, Angel crashed into the ground.

A sharp impact ran through his whole body as though he had been thrown off of a horse, and Angel began to lose consciousness.

"Angel! Get up!!"

He jumped up at Jorge's bellowed command but was immediately assaulted by severe pain. He felt like all the bones in his body were being ground into dust.

"Gah…"

Angel curled up and tried to fight off the pain.

It was a nightmare situation, but he had managed not to break any bones at least. He had been three meters in the air when he fell and merely had his body slammed. He might have still cracked a few bones but was able to move.

Next step, allowing the use of both controllers alongside your weapon…

Angel forced himself to laugh, then got up by using his short sword as a cane. The incredible pain that ran through his body was almost enough to make him scream, but he bore it.

Once he checked his surroundings, he immediately understood his situation. He had collapsed within the soldiers' circular formation, in other words, by the Titan's feet. It was not luck that had kept him from being stepped on, but the soldiers' constant attacks against the Titan's legs. Other soldiers' carbines were firing a hail of bullets at the Titan's torso, which was why he hadn't grabbed Angel.

Why couldn't I kill it?

Angel looked up at the Titan and combed back over what he knew.

The Titans can be killed. I'm certain of that.

But the Titan was still standing, even though Angel had attacked the weak point.

That means their weakness isn't their throat.

It had to be in that area, though.

What was it that Solm did?

Angel balked at rehashing the terrible memory, but he dredged it up nevertheless. Solm had intentionally held grenades in his hand and blown himself up in order to let the others get away. He must have judged that hurling them might not slow down the Titan. To make sure, he'd grabbed onto the nape and blown the Titan's head off. Although the creatures did not expire from losing a portion of their bodies, it limited their movements until they regenerated. In fact, it was thanks to the troops neutralizing the Titan's physical capacities that Angel hadn't been stepped on.

But the Titan whose head we blew off still didn't die.

In other words, destroying their head only limited their capacity to act. It wasn't their weakness.

That only leaves one place.

Angel looked toward the Titan's nape, but he was too close to see it. When he thought back, that was where Solm had grabbed onto when he blew himself up. During their behavioral study, it was the only area they hadn't destroyed. The horrible sight of a Titan's brains scattering had distracted them enough to gloss over a crucial point.

The Titan stomped on the ground in what seemed like anger at being used as target practice for so long. The impact was like a direct hit from a cannon, rumbling through the soldiers' feet and making it impossible to stay standing. It surprised the horses, who ran wild and scattered the formation.

"Angel, come back! We're retreating!" Jorge yelled, apparently having judged that the situation had turned sour.

But Angel saw it as an opportunity. He returned his short sword to its scabbard and took controllers in both hands. Checking them, he found them to be fully functional. He had gas left, too. As soon as he confirmed this, he pointed his left controller at the Titan and shot an anchor into the abdomen, quickly pulling himself up. Next, he used his right controller to aim for the chest. By using both controllers in tandem, he soared up to the Titan's eyes. The problem was how he would get around to the creature's back.

Vertical movement isn't enough. I need to be able to move in all three dimensions.

Through this battle Angel had discovered a number of ways to improve the Equipment, but it was not the time to be occupied with them. With both hands taken up by controllers, there was no way for him to attack, either.

Then I'll just have to use this thing!

Angel shot an anchor into the Titan's right eye, steadied his body, then visited the left eye with the other. Even Titans had to come to a grinding halt when their vision was taken away.

Yet, perhaps peeved that his eyes had been crushed, the Titan began shaking his head from side to side like an obstinate child. Angel's body swung in arcs as a result. The centrifugal force nearly caused the anchors to fall out, but Angel used it to his advantage. It allowed him to move horizontally in a way that the Equipment did not and to circle around to the Titan's back. Angel quickly reeled his wires in, clung to the Titan's nape, and drew his short sword out from its scabbard.

"It ends here!"

Angel forcefully cut into the Titan's nape, but the weakened blade could not stand the impact, splitting cleanly in two with a high-pitched sound.

"Now of all times…"

Angel clicked his tongue, but he still had another option. He could expect to do a significant amount of damage if he detonated the grenades he carried. That had been Solm's method; at the same time, Angel didn't intend to blow himself up along with the Titan. The problem was that he faced a ten-plus-meter-class monster, which meant he might be short on firepower. Even if he were to fire the flare gun along with the grenades, he could only do so much damage, but he had no other explosives.

We'll just have to try and see.

As he reached for a controller, Angel suddenly realized it.

They're certainly explosive.

The cylinders he wore on his hips. They were both full of gas, and if he could detonate them along with the grenades, it would likely be enough to do the job. He would lose the Equipment's fuel, but he could manually extend the wires, and that would be enough.

Angel took both of his cylinders off, stuck them in the Titan's wound, and began to release the gas they held. Next, he grabbed the grenades he carried on his hip, pulled the safety pins, and tossed them inside. All that was left was to jump off to avoid being caught by the explosion. Angel grabbed his controllers, kicked off from the Titan's body, and dived into the air.

A moment later—

The grenades exploded with a radiant flash, setting off the cylinders in turn. The Titan's nape was blown off, sending chunks of meat and bone and bodily fluids in every direction. As this happened, a dark red flame engulfed the Titan's head.

Everything was going as planned so far, but having detonated grenades and gas at a close distance, Angel had to worry about himself. A shockwave surged toward him, and with it a gust of hot air. He had neither the time nor the means to protect himself, and his senses wavered upon taking the full brunt of the impact. He felt as though the hot air was scorching his body hair and heard crackles all around his body. Sunburn-like pain radiated from his exposed skin, but he paid no mind as he continued to watch the Titan. Something seemed to cause the hot air around the Titan to shimmer hazily, perhaps the explosion or the heat it gave off. Soon, the haze turned to fog and began covering the Titan's body.

"The Titan… He's disappearing…"

Angel felt light just as he noticed this. The anchors must have come unstuck from the Titan's body as it grew unstable. Angel's body was pulled back toward the ground.

"See? You *can* kill Titans…"

Angel grinned.

EPILOGUE

A sharp pain ran through Angel's body, suddenly bringing him back to reality from the depths of a deep slumber. His body ached from his head to his toes, making it a chore to budge a single finger. Moving his body was out of the question, and he didn't even have the energy to open his eyes and look around.

"Are you up?"

The male voice was familiar. "Jorge…"

"Looks like you're still alive."

"Just barely."

Angel could manage to banter, but the pain he felt with every word he spoke twisted his face.

"We'll be back in town soon. I know it's not a comfortable ride, but try to bear it."

Apparently strapped onto the horse that Jorge was riding, Angel's body bounced rhythmically with its movements.

"What…happened to me?"

"You don't remember?"

"I remember blowing the Titan up."

He'd blacked out before he could see the end result, but everything must have gone according to plan if he was now having a conversation with Jorge. Angel was still alive thanks to what could only be described as a stroke of incredible luck.

"You proved that the Titans can be killed."

"Their weakness was their nape, though."

He'd nearly died because of that, but he was satisfied with the result.

Still, there were many challenges ahead. The short sword's durability, the simultaneous use of a weapon with both controllers, and the Equipment's mobility. They may have proven that Titans could be killed, but a pile of issues still had to be resolved.

They also had to zero in on the Titans' weakness. Defeating one was not enough. They needed to look into why the Titan had died, which would require continued surveys.

Establishing tactics that employed the Equipment was also necessary. Reaching the Titans' weak point in the fastest and shortest way and delivering a decisive blow—fumbling as Angel had would exact an unacceptable toll in lives. The Equipment had to be improved, of course, but if they could all master it, they could even start hunting the Titans.

"Things are going to get hectic for the Survey Corps."

"Yes. In a lot of ways."

It was very likely that the dissolution of the Survey Corps would be rescinded now that they had proved that the Titans could be defeated. On the other hand, they had ignored orders and gone on an expedition. Putting aside what would happen to the rank and file, as commander, Jorge would have to take responsibility for his actions. It seemed inevitable that he would have to resign.

"There's something I need to do," the commander said.

"What's that?"

"Bring up the next generation."

"By training recruits or something?"

"It needs doing, don't you think?"

"Yeah, true."

The Survey Corps' numbers had been drastically reduced. Training recruits and thus rebuilding the Survey Corps could be Jorge's next calling.

But Jorge was looking at the situation in a slightly different way.

"When I saw you fight, I knew the age for soldiers like me had come to an end."

"You're making it sound like I'm the one putting you out of commission…"

"I think that's exactly what happened."

"Isn't that a little overblown?"

There was no question about Jorge's abilities, and the same went for those under him. The commander was surely still capable of shining in combat, and they needed him to.

"The way we fight is going to change radically because of that device you made. I don't know about the younger men and women, but personally, it's too late for me to change my fighting style."

"And that's why you're stepping down? I gotta say, I do find that gracious," Angel replied with honest admiration. "Becoming a training instructor might be the right choice."

Training the next generation still meant developing soldiers' minds, bodies, and skills. Jorge was the perfect man for the job. Angel could already picture Jorge throwing trainees through the mill. If a veteran like him who knew the Titans inside and out became an instructor, he'd start churning out the greatest soldiers they'd ever seen.

"If they're going to master that device, they need to be taught how to use it from the time they're recruits."

"And you're offering to do that?"

"Good idea, isn't it?"

"I need to get started on improving the Equipment." But Angel wouldn't be able to do it overnight. His head hurt when he thought about the mountain of issues he faced.

"Is that its official name? 'Equipment'?"

"It's just what I call it. It's more like a code name. I didn't think up a real name because it's a prototype."

Now that he could see the Equipment coming to completion, though, a name wouldn't hurt.

"Hmm…" Angel thought for a while as he tried to come up with something that reflected the Equipment's unique traits. "Well, it's equipment that allows for vertical movement, so maybe the Vertical Maneuvering Equipment."

"Ah, not bad."

"I still have to make them, of course."

Angel managed to laugh and pulled his leaden eyelids open. His blazing and aching eyes filled with tears. His entire body was covered in injuries, and his eyes were no exception. His vision was dim and unclear as though he were looking through frosted glass.

That must've been when.

His eyes must have been scorched by hot wind as he watched the Titan's final moments.

I've done something, though, haven't I?

He didn't know if his vision would recover, but he felt full of satisfaction.

"The hero returns," Jorge proudly proclaimed.

Angel heard the sound of the main gate opening.

THE END

AFTERWORD

Kodansha first contacted me in the summer of last year, which means it's been a year and a half in total… Writing this afterword is starting to make me reminisce.

You know, back then, the Kodansha Lightnovel editorial department was still called the "light novel research department." It was full of veteran editors, and I wondered what they'd need to research at that point in their careers, but it looks like the line managed to launch, which is the most important thing of all.

Anyway, I'm Suzukaze.

If this is our first meeting, nice to meet you. If not, it's good to see you again. Did you enjoy *Attack on Titan: Before the Fall*?

It was a year and a half ago when my editor asked me, "Is there something you want to do?" and I answered, "*Attack on Titan*." The situation around *Attack on Titan* has changed drastically since then, hasn't it. Really by leaps and bounds as they say.

I personally first learned about *Attack on Titan* through a tweet made by a Twitter follower. Someone important at a certain video game company in Hakata tweeted, "I'm enjoying *Attack on Titan*," so I figured I'd buy it.

I don't think I need to tell you my reaction. It was practically a given that I'd answer "*Attack on Titan*" to the question "What do you want to do?" And anyway, pitches alone don't cost anything! (lol)

I think it also helped that the content of the story makes it well-suited for a novelization.

Okay. About *Attack on Titan: Before the Fall*. It's what you'd imagine it to be from the subtitle.

The end.

…But leaving it at that wouldn't do at all, so I'll go over it a bit, without spoiling anything in case you're reading this afterword first. As the subtitle, *Before the Fall*, indicates, this story takes place before the original story, or before Wall Maria falls.

It's wintertime for humanity, as they are in a situation where the Vertical Maneuvering Equipment doesn't exist and they have no set tactics for fighting against the Titans. For the Survey Corps, expeditions are like trips to go meet death, and the Titans are nightmares incarnate. Personally, I don't think I'd live in Shiganshina District. I'd live closer to the interior in Trost District, but I digress.

In this book, I tried to bring readers to the world of *Attack on Titan* from a slightly different angle as compared to the original by doing things like making the protagonist, Angel, a craftsman of arms. It explains the inner workings of things such as materials, manufacturing processes, facilities, and so on.

What personally stands out to me is the material known as Iron Bamboo in the book. As for how it's used, please read the book if you haven't yet…

I was reminded of how I used to play with bamboo as a child. I'd pretend sword-fight with small bamboo, make bamboo-copters, and build piggy banks out of bamboo. I'd break open my banks almost immediately, of course, but it was all fun in its own way. I never went as far as digging up bamboo shoots, though.

With bamboo appearing in my story, I thought it'd be nice to visit a bamboo grove, but alas, unsurprisingly I couldn't find one in my neighborhood… Or so you'd think, but on my jogging course I came across a place where some grew on a modest scale. It became a basic reference for me as I worked on my manuscript. Mosquitoes brutally assaulted me as a result, but at least I didn't run into any Titan attacks.

Oops, got off track again.

There are a few other items that I should talk about here, but please find them in the story. You can probably spot and compare some things in the manga that are brought up in this book, and vice versa.

I went into a lot of detail about it, but one item I hope you pay special attention to is the Vertical Maneuvering Equipment. Without it, *Attack on Titan* would never get off the ground.

While Eren and Mikasa probably won't learn about Angel, a mere craftsman, the fact that the two are active in the way they are is surely enough to satisfy him.

All right. I've wasted too much space and I'm running out of lines, so before I forget, I'd like to give thanks to a few people involved in this production.

Thank you, Isayama-sama, for bringing the world the incredible title that is *Attack on Titan*, and for your permission for this novelization.

Thank you, THORES Shibamoto-sama, for adorning this title with the flowers that are your illustrations. It seems as though you're still drawing the insert illustrations, so please do your best (I know, this isn't the place to say it).

Kodachi-sama, Miwa-sama, the story lore you laid out for me was extremely helpful. Thank you very much!

Nabae-sama and Fujita-sama from Kodansha Lightnovel, I'm looking forward to continuing to work with you.

Finally, my greatest thanks to all of you who read this book. If you have any thoughts, please send them through the editorial department, or send them to me on Twitter. I'll probably read them. I don't tweet much myself, but if you're interested, you can follow me at @suzukazeR.

Until next time!

October 26, 2011 (the day of the first cold breeze of the season)
Ryo Suzukaze

Knights of Sidonia

TSUTOMU NIHEI

CORE EXPOSED

Outer space, the far future.

A lone seed ship, the *Sidonia*, plies the void, ten centuries since the obliteration of the solar system. The massive, nearly indestructible, yet barely sentient alien life forms that destroyed humanity's home world continue to pose an existential threat.

Nagate Tanikaze has only known life in the vessel's bowels deep below the sparkling strata where humans have achieved photosynthesis and new genders. Not long after he emerges from the Underground, however, the youth is bequeathed a treasured legacy by the spaceship's coolheaded female captain.

Meticulously drawn, peppered with clipped humor, but also unusually attentive to plot and structure for the international cult favorite, *Knights of Sidonia* may be Tsutomu Nihei's most accessible work to date even as it hits notes of tragic grandeur as a hopeless struggle for survival unfolds.

A SEARING MANGA FOR SCI-FI AND *ATTACK ON TITAN* FANS! VOLUMES 1-10 AVAILABLE NOW!!

THE GUIN SAGA

KAORU KURIMOTO

In a single day and night of fierce
fighting, the Archduchy of Mongaul has
overrun its elegant neighbor, Parros. The lost
priest kingdom's surviving royalty, the young twins Rinda
and Remus, hide in a forest in the forbidding wild marches.
There they are saved by a mysterious creature with a man's
body and a leopard's head, who has just emerged from a deep
sleep and remembers only his name. Guin.

A key precursor of the light novel style, Kaoru Kurimoto's
lifework will enthrall readers of all ages with its universal themes,
uncommon richness, and otherworldly intrigue.

Visit us at www.vertical-inc.com for a teaser chapter!